REASONS TO RESIST

Lady Sarah Wyndham had every reason to find the
Viscount Jethro Newsome as despicable as he was
demanding.

He came out of nowhere to seize her beloved
Mansfield manor, and to exile her to a far more
humble dwelling. He took total command of the
servants who had once been at her beck and call.
And he accused her to her face of being faithless
to the late husband to whom she had been so loyal.

Sarah had every good reason to resist Jethro, and a
stunning secret weapon to win back all he had taken
from her. But the heart had its reasons, too . . .
reasons as strong and as weak as love . . . .

IRENE SAUNDERS, a native of Yorkshire, England,
worked a number of years for the U.S. Air Force in
London. A love of travel brought her to New York City,
where she met her husband, Ray. She now lives in Port St.
Lucie, Florida, dividing her time between writing, book-
keeping, gardening, needlepoint, and travel.

THE
DOWAGER'S DILEMMA

Irene Saunders

A SIGNET BOOK

SIGNET
Published by the Penguin Group
Penguin Books USA Inc., 375 Hudson Street,
New York, New York, 10014, U.S.A.
Penguin Books Ltd, 27 Wrights Lane, London W8 5TZ, England
Penguin Books Australia Ltd, Ringwood, Victoria, Australia
Penguin Books Canada Ltd, 2801 John Street,
Markham, Ontario, Canada L3R 1B4
Penguin Books (N.Z.) Ltd, 182-190 Wairau Road,
Auckland 10, New Zealand

Penguin Books Ltd, Registered Offices:
Harmondsworth, Middlesex, England

First published by Signet, an imprint of New American Library,
a division of Penguin Books USA Inc.

First Printing, May, 1991

10 9 8 7 6 5 4 3 2 1

 REGISTERED TRADEMARK—MARCA REGISTRADA

PRINTED IN THE UNITED STATES OF AMERICA

1

Shortly before two o'clock on a wintry afternoon in March, the late Lord Wyndham's solicitor, a Mr. Samuel Musgrave, related the shockingly disappointing contents of his client's will to the young widow and her older brother—a clear case for not putting off until tomorrow what should have been done today.

"I find it quite impossible to believe, sir, that the earl had made no provision whatsoever for my sister," Lord Pelham said in stunned surprise. "Surely the dowry she brought with her a year and a half ago is still intact, for Lord Wyndham admitted he had little need of it himself."

"I clearly recall suggesting that Lord Wyndham make the dowry part of a trust for our daughters, Rob," the young widow said quietly, "so it might take some time to obtain it. Is that not true, Mr. Musgrave?"

The quite ancient gentleman, who was seated behind the handsome oak desk that had served the earl and his father before him, had always personally attended to their affairs and was now decidedly uncomfortable. He coughed several times, then cleared his throat before slowly intoning, "That is so, my lady, and I am sure it was never his intention to leave you without a suitable jointure." His watery eyes held a hint of apology for allowing such an oversight. "You see, he was still a comparatively young man and was quite determined that sons—and daughters too, of course—would soon be forthcoming. Had that been the case, as one of the guardians of your children, you would have been amply provided for.

"I cannot but feel sure, however, that the heir, when made aware of your unusual position, will be most generous in this matter, and, of course, there is the priory, which has always served as the dower house."

Sarah Wyndham had been completely shocked by her husband's sudden demise. Despite more than twenty years' difference in their ages, she had been fond of him and their marriage had been a reasonably happy one.

She was attired in a simple black bombazine gown which, though obviously not made for her in the style and fit of her London modiste, was nonetheless most attractive on her still-youthful figure. Her eyes, held by many of her former suitors to be her most outstanding feature, were now shadowed, but there was no mistaking the intelligence in their gray depths. Dark brown hair framed a face that was paler today than usual, and though her chin was resolute, her soft lips parted slightly as she could not help but shudder at the thought of living in a house she had always considered to be no better than a mausoleum.

Her brother was quick to notice.

"It's not that bad a place, old girl," he told her, "though it's a little noisy at the moment, with the whole family staying there. I've no doubt Adele will help you fix it up to your liking."

Sarah looked at him as if he was about in the head. "It is not my intention to move from the manor just yet, Rob, for someone must be here to keep things running as they should. Even the best of servants neglect their duties when unsupervised. When I asked for your help, it was because I felt obligated to maintain the house and estates in as good order as possible until Percy's heir finally gets here. I did not mean, however, that you should bring our stepmama and the rest of the family with you," she added, her fine dark brows drawing together in a frown.

Robert grinned. "Took you aback a little, I've no doubt, when you saw the old coach piled high with baggage. For a moment there you looked completely flabbergasted."

"I was," she readily admitted, "and I can only believe that Adele meant it for the best, though it has but added to my worries. Young Bryan reminds me of you at the same age, constantly up to some mischief or other. And Meg is going through that awkward time when she is no longer a child nor yet a lady."

Sarah suddenly became aware that the solicitor was patiently waiting to finish explaining the steps he had taken. "I'm sorry, Mr. Musgrave. Pray continue, and do tell me everything you know of Viscount Newsome so that I may be as prepared as possible."

The old gentleman slowly shook his head. "I'm afraid we know almost nothing about him, my lady, except that he is unmarried, now in his thirtieth year, and cannot be lacking in either intelligence or leadership, for he has attained the rank of colonel under Wellington. Word of Lord Percy's death will be as much of a surprise to him, I am sure, as it was to my esteemed colleagues and myself. As to when you may expect him, I doubt he'll be here in less than two months, for it may take quite some time for my missive to reach him." He paused, smiling a little helplessly. "Then again, we may be fortunate and have the young earl with us in a month."

Turning to her brother, Sarah asked, "Can you remain here so long, Rob? I'd be more than grateful if you could possibly see your way to doing so, for I know so little about the lands themselves, and the men who worked for Percy."

Lord Pelham nodded. He was a serious young man of twenty-four years, who had inherited the rank of baron from their father. He was by nature more practical and methodical than Sarah, and though nothing was settled as yet, he had a suitable young lady already picked out to be his wife.

"I must return home for a day or two next week, and then every fortnight or so, but I'll be here as much as I can to help you," he promised. "Can't let the fellow's inheritance go to rack and ruin before he even sets eyes on it."

Mr. Musgrave started to gather together his papers in preparation for his departure. "If there is anything I can do to ease your burden, my lady, please do not hesitate to get in touch with me," he murmured.

"Surely you'll stay and have tea with us before you start back to town?" Sarah suggested, but the old gentleman shook his head.

"Thank you kindly, my lady, but I'd best be off, for with the dreadful things that go on these days, I do dislike traveling country roads after dark," he told her, then added once more, "but you must not forget, if I can be of further service, you have only to send word."

Lord Pelham walked to the door with the older man, and assisted him into his carriage; then he returned to the library and took a chair across from his sister.

"It's a sorry state of affairs, to be sure, and I can't think what either Percy or Mr. Musgrave was about to overlook something so important," he said, shaking his head. "It's to be hoped that the new earl is a decent sort of fellow and will realize Percy just didn't think of it."

"I can't be cross with Percy, for I know he didn't mean things to turn out this way. We'd already had a few false starts, you know, and he was sure that the next time I'd truly be increasing," Sarah said a little sadly, for she, also, had wished for a child.

"Adele is going to be quite devastated when she learns that you have not been amply provided for. She had hopes of your bringing young Margaret out in town a year from now, I believe," Robert remarked. "However, I cannot but think that Newsome will take care of such an omission as soon as he gets here, though it is doubtful that, not knowing you, he will be as generous as Percy."

There was a knock on the door and Rivers, the austere butler who had also served Percy's father, entered.

"Mrs. Pennyfarthing asked if you might like tea now, milady," he intoned, his face carefully devoid of expression, "and if we are to expect the young people to be present also?"

Sarah suddenly wondered what her young half-brother, Bryan, had been doing, for she had neither seen nor heard from him all day. "I should think they will, Rivers, unless Bryan is down at the stream again, trying to catch trout with his hands."

The butler shook his head. "I believe he is, at the moment, on his way to the priory to change his clothes, milady."

"Where was he this time, Rivers?" Lord Pelham asked wearily.

"In the attics, milord, looking for fishing rods."

"Oh, dear." Sarah smiled, for she now had a very good idea of the condition Bryan must be in. "There have to be rods somewhere, Rob, for Percy taught me how to fish when we first came here after our wedding trip, and we used rods he had fished with here as a boy."

"The young gentleman did discover them, milady, and also uncovered a great deal of dust." There was now a glint of humor in Rivers' eyes. "I'll tell Cook that he will be returning."

When the door had closed, Lord Pelham turned to his sister. "What was that all about?" he asked. "Is Bryan making a nuisance of himself again?"

"He's never seen trout swimming in a stream before, and he's very eager to learn how to catch them. You must be quite devastated, I am sure, that you are no fisherman." Sarah's eyes sparkled with fun. "I'll try to find out if any of the footmen or grooms can give him a few lessons. It would, at least, keep him out of mischief for an hour or two. Come along and let's see if Adele and Aunt Agatha are in the drawing room as yet."

The two older ladies were indeed there, and at least one of them was waiting impatiently to ascertain what the solicitor might have revealed, but, as seventeen-year-old Margaret was with them, any discussion of the will had to be postponed until after they had all partaken of numerous cups of oolong tea and a number of the delicate cakes and pastries Cook felt were essential to sustain them all until dinner.

Bryan was late, of course, but he more than made up for his tardiness by ensuring that there was little in the way of food to take back to the kitchen. Then, once the remains of tea were cleared away, he and Margaret were sent back to the priory.

Lady Pelham leaned forward in the wing chair she had chosen, eager to hear what the solicitor had revealed. She was a widow in her mid-forties, who had once been quite attractive, with fine hazel eyes and dark brown curls, but her hair had now turned to a salt-and-pepper shade and her eyes had become lined as she tried to cope with the numerous problems of widowhood. She had brought up her husband's motherless children to the best of her ability, from the ages of six and eight years, and now had high hopes that her stepdaughter's position as the dowager Countess of Mansfield would help secure good marriages for her own two youngsters.

"We saw the old gentleman leave," she said brightly. "Was he able to tell you when the new earl will be coming, my dear? I know so well how you must feel about someone taking your dear husband's place, but that is the way of our world, I'm afraid."

Sarah looked across at her brother and nodded for him to make the explanations.

"The heir is a Viscount Jethro Newsome," Robert began, "who is presently serving under Wellington on the Peninsula. Word has been sent to him, but it will probably be some time before he receives it and, presumably, either buys out or returns to take a look at his inheritance."

"And what is to happen to Sarah in the meantime?" Lady

Pelham asked sharply, turning to her stepdaughter. "Must you retire to the dower house at once, my dear?"

"I have no intention of leaving the manor until the heir arrives, for there is much to do here in order to maintain things in the way my husband was used to," Sarah declared flatly. "I believe it would be best if I go along as I have been doing for now. Robert must return home to take care of a few matters and will then come back to help me. How long do you mean to remain here, Adele? Will you go back with him?"

"I would not even think of leaving you alone so soon after your loss, my dear Sarah. We will all remain here for the time being, but if we're to stay at the priory, we really must have extra help. Did you decide which servants you will take when you move there permanently?" Lady Pelham asked, frowning.

"It's difficult for Sarah to make any decisions at present," Robert interposed. "You see, the late earl neglected to make specific provisions for Sarah, so she has no alternative but to wait and see what the new earl means to do."

Lady Pelham looked completely shocked. "What are you saying, Robert? Surely Percy set aside monies for his widow's use, for I never heard of anyone not doing so."

Sarah smiled and said quietly, "It's nothing to worry about at the moment, Adele. Should the new earl be delayed more than a month or so, the solicitors will make necessary payments on his behalf. Then, once he gets here, no matter what he is like, he will hardly leave me to starve," she added dryly.

"I should think not," Lady Pelham asserted, now extremely concerned for her own plans. "I just hope he's not clutch-fisted, for at your age you'll have to start looking for another husband once the year of mourning is over, and you'll need ample funds in order to make the best appearance. What happened to your dowry?"

Robert frowned, then said sternly, "This is hardly the time to speak of such things, Adele, My sister is in need of our comfort and support. Discussion at this time of her seeking another husband is in the worst possible taste. I'll be going home next week for a day or two. If you should change your mind about remaining here, you may, of course, return with me."

Lady Pelham's chin rose and her lips pursed at the rebuke. "I journeyed here at considerable inconvenience, in order, as you say, Robert, to give Sarah my comfort and support. It is not my intention to leave before the new earl arrives and I am able to see for myself the kind of man she will be forced to depend upon. Before you go, however, I will give you a list of things to bring back with you," Lady Pelham pronounced, then added, "Your criticism is grossly unfair, to say the least, for I have been like Sarah's own mother to her, and I mean to see that she is treated the way I know that Percy intended. I can see him now, when he used to come courting Sarah, with his hair as red as a carrot and a twinkle in those bright green eyes. Such a handsome gentleman!"

Sarah listened without comment to her stepmother's remarks, then turned to Lady Agatha Ramsbottom, who, though now approaching seventy years, sat tall and stately in a large Egyptian-style armchair, her cane in her hand.

Speaking in a slightly louder tone, for the old lady did not always catch what was said to her these days, Sarah asked, "How are you managing at the priory, Aunt Agatha? Are you quite comfortable, and is everything to your liking?"

"I quite like the place. It's so old, my dear, that it makes me feel young again," Lady Agatha said with a chuckle, her watery blue eyes twinkling. "Did you know there's supposed to be a ghost in residence?"

"Now, I'm sure you don't believe anything of that sort," Sarah said, smiling fondly at the old lady. "But you'd best not let Bryan hear about it or he'll be waiting up to try to catch a glimpse of it next full moon."

"So you are aware of the tale, then," Aunt Agatha said,

"for I made no mention just now that it's seen only at full moon."

"Of course I am," Sarah said with a smile, "but I 've never yet met anyone who has seen it. The place really was a priory once, you know, and the ghost is supposed to be one of the monks, complete with cloak and hood, who at times gets a little restless and prowls around. After the priory was no longer used, it fell into disrepair and one of Percy's ancestors restored it to use as a dower house, for he felt it was just the right distance from the manor."

Lady Pelham interrupted. "I've never heard of anything so ridiculous. Ghosts indeed! If Bryan does hear of it, we'll have no peace, for he'll be up all night trying to scare first one and another of us."

"Oh, you can be sure he's heard already," Robert said with a grin, "and is simply biding his time."

"It just occurred to me," Lady Pelham said brightly, "that if the new earl is unlikely to be here for a month, there's no reason why we should not all remove ourselves here and leave the priory to the ghost. It would be much more comfortable and . . ."

Her voice tapered off as Sarah firmly shook her head. "Mansfield Manor now belongs to the earl, whether he is here or not, and I mean to spend the next few weeks in seeing that it is cleaned from attics to cellars," she announced, though she did not add that the idea had only just entered her head. "I shall be turning out all of the bedchambers, leaving my own to the very last. And I mean to do the same with the downstairs rooms except for the dining room, where we may all have dinner together each evening. That, too, will be left until last. I'll have the assistant cook come to you at the priory to prepare breakfast and a light nuncheon each day, but I must keep the rest of the servants here to give this house the cleaning it is so badly in need of. I don't believe it has been done since Percy's first wife died."

Lady Pelham seemed about to protest, then decided against

it and shrugged slightly. Sarah was being practical for a change, for if the size of her allowance depended upon the new earl's generosity, then she must do all in her power to please him until the arrangements were agreed upon.

There was no opportunity to discuss the matter further that evening, for the two younger children were present, but early the next morning Sarah was as good as her word and started supervising the most thorough going-over the house had known in years.

In view of Sarah's decision, Robert left earlier than he had planned, and when he returned a few days later, it was to find the manor a hive of activity. He finally ran his sister to earth in one of the attics, where she was sorting through the accumulation of toys, furniture, paintings, and trunks to decide what was worth saving, what might be used in the priory, and what should be thrown away.

"I just spoke to Adele and she said you looked a little down-pin, and now I know why," he told her. "You'd best leave this to Mrs. Pennyfarthing now, and come with me to the library, for there's much to do if you mean to have the estates in good order for the earl's arrival."

Lady Pelham had the right of it, for once. Sarah did feel a little out of sorts, but was trying hard to ignore it. She had never been subject to dizzy spells, but had experienced two in the last few days and put them down to some of the accumulation of dust getting into her lungs. She was glad of the excuse to tidy herself up and join her brother in the sparklingly clean library, which had been the first room to be turned out.

"So far as I can see," Robert remarked, "things run pretty smoothly here as a rule, or at least they did until the earl's accident. This last week or so, however, Bennett, the bailiff, has become somewhat lax, and I've asked him to join us in half an hour to tell me why some of the work appears to have slowed down, if not quite come to a halt."

Sarah looked surprised. "He seemed such an eager, conscientious man," she murmured, "and he promised me that everything would go on exactly as it did when the late earl was alive.''

Robert shrugged. "He may, perhaps, believe it himself, but few men work as hard when there's no one to watch what they're doing. Now, before he gets here, let me go over with you the work I'll be talking to him about, so that you'll have a better understanding of what is going on."

Sarah quickly understood the situation, and had naught but admiration for the way her brother dealt pleasantly but firmly with Bennett, finally going off with him to see some of the work for himself while Sarah stayed behind to go over the books, as she had frequently been doing since her husband's death. She became so immersed in the details of the various ledgers and accounts that she was surprised when she heard Robert's voice and looked up as Rivers entered to ask if he should send in afternoon tea.

"Tea and a few scones will do, and we'll have it over there," she told him, pointing to a couch near the bay window.

When he had left, she rose and stretched her cramped muscles, and Robert, who had entered in the meanwhile, remarked with a grin, "So this is where you've been hiding from our stepmama. She told me, in the most aggrieved tones, that she tried to call on you one afternoon just after I left, and was informed that you did not wish to be disturbed during the day—that you would discuss anything important before dinner each evening. Is she getting to be a little too much for you?"

"They all are, Rob, except, perhaps, Aunt Agatha," she told him. "You see, I'm no longer accustomed to having so many disruptive people around me all day. Bryan and Meg are constantly quarreling, and Adele can think of little else save finding a suitable husband for Meg. She is already hinting to use the Mansfield town house next Season, as though I will have anything to say in the matter! I'm a little ashamed to admit that dinner each evening is just about as much of their company as I can tolerate at the moment.''

"You mustn't mind Adele," her brother said gently. "She's not a bad sort, and it's only natural that she should have the interests of her own children at heart. Should I be gone, however, when the new earl finally arrives, you'd best keep them separated. She's never been known for her tact, and she might make him jump to entirely the wrong conclusions. Don't let her bedevil you now, for you've handled her very well indeed so far. By the way, your decision to clean this place from top to bottom the minute she expressed the wish to move in was quite masterly."

Sarah nodded and grinned a little sheepishly, for these last few days she had frequently come to much the same conclusion.

"I believe I shall be glad to see the new earl get here at last," Sarah said with a sigh, "for if he doesn't come soon, I'll be worn to a shadow with all the work."

2

The journey had been long and wearying for the officer traveling ahead on horseback, with his batman and baggage a half-day behind, but his instincts told him that he was almost at his destination. The light was fast fading, and at this distance he could not quite read the sign swinging to and fro outside the inn he was approaching. He felt sure, however, that it must be the Hooded Monk, mentioned in the solicitor's letter.

He rode into the yard but did not dismount when a stableboy hurried forward, for it was not his intent to stop here, but to press on to his destination.

"Point the way to Mansfield Manor for me, lad," he called gruffly, tossing the boy a coin. The youngster eagerly ran ahead to show him the country lane that would take him there.

Now that he neared the end of his journey, he slowed his pace, as he had no wish to lame his horse in a rabbit hole. He was still in uniform, for though he had at once expressed the wish to sell out upon receiving the solicitor's letter, Wellington would have none of it. Instead, he had told him to first take a leave of absence, return to England and see for himself just what was included in his cousin's entailed property, and then decide if it was indeed worth the giving up of a promising army career.

News of his cousin's sudden death had profoundly shocked him. He remembered Percy as being about ten years or so his elder, and most anxious to start a family of his own, but it would seem his cousin's wish had not been granted.

There would have been some merit, of course, in his spending the night in London and meeting on the morrow with Mr. Musgrave, the solicitor who had conveyed the news, but then, a day would have been wasted, and he was not one to waste either time or words.

The land on either side of the lane must be his cousin's, he decided—or rather his own land now, though he could not yet bring himself to think of it as such. Reining in, he gazed with awe at the noble residence in the distance that one of his forebears had chosen to call a manor.

The last rays of a pale, wintry sky were casting but a faint glow over the golden stone and reflecting softly on the forty or more windows in the front of the house, yet its magnificence was difficult to believe. He had never dreamed of owning anything of such proportions, and hoped with all his heart that it might not be mortgaged to the hilt and become a millstone around his neck.

He went first to the stables, for he felt that the gelding was more in need of attention than he. His dusty scarlet uniform caused an obvious stir, and the head groom hurriedly escorted him to the front of the house and clanged the bell loudly until a footman threw open the big door.

"Be ye trying to waken the dead?" the footman started to ask, then gazed transfixed at the uniformed officer. He realized at once who the soldier must be, for there had been little else talked of belowstairs in the past month or more.

Rivers hurried forward then, for a stableboy had raced through from the back of the house to let him know of the new master's unorthodox arrival.

"Welcome, milord," he said with a bow. "Allow me to show you into the drawing room. Lady Wyndham will be with you in a moment, I am sure."

Jethro smiled and nodded. "Thank you, and you are . . .?" he asked.

"Rivers, milord," the butler said, then added with a note of pride in his voice, "butler to the late earl and also to his father before him."

Jethro nodded and walked over to a portrait of Percy that hung over the mantelpiece. It was exactly the way he remembered him, and must have been painted about the time they had last met.

At the sound of a quick, light step in the hall he swung around and looked in surprise at a young lady, gowned in deepest black, who came toward him and dropped a curtsy. Taking her hand, he gazed into a pair of soft gray eyes above a mouth that he felt sure had been meant for only one thing. This was neither the time nor the place, however, and he waited eagerly to find out who this charming creature might be—a niece, perhaps, or sister of the widow.

"I am the dowager Lady Wyndham, my lord. Percy's wife. Do you not think that an excellent portrait of him?" she asked a little breathlessly, for she had been changing for dinner when Rivers sent word, and had quickly donned her gown and hurried down to greet him.

"Most certainly, my lady," he murmured, but his expression was one of puzzlement. "You cannot possibly be the wife Percy was married to when last I saw him, for you're not old enough."

Her cheeks went a rosy pink. "No, I'm not. We were married some eighteen months ago, when he had been a widower for almost two years," she explained a little awkwardly. Then she recalled the reason she had hurried to greet him. "We keep country hours and have dinner, as a rule, in about fifteen minutes. The master bedroom is already prepared for you, so if you would like a half-hour or more to wash off the dust of the road, we'll be glad to wait."

He grinned, pleased that she was not a dissembler. "My

batman is still a day behind me," he said quietly, "but if Percy's valet is here and can give me a hand, I'll keep you no more than thirty minutes, for I've not eaten since early morning."

While he was being shown to his bedchamber, Sarah made arrangements for the simple meal to be augmented somewhat, and delayed, then returned to her bedchamber for Betty to put the finishing touches to her toilette before making her way to the dining room to face five pairs of questioning eyes. Lady Pelham was the first to speak.

"Well, what is he like, my dear? Does he seem to be an agreeable type of person?" she asked anxiously.

"He's a big man, tall, with broad shoulders, and even with his scarlet coat covered in dust, he made a most impressive appearance," Sarah told them, remembering how imposing he had seemed when she rose from her curtsy, and the little tug of attraction she had felt when their eyes met. "He has black hair, and very blue eyes, and he must stand at least six feet. He is also very hungry and will be joining us in less than fifteen minutes now, so you had best watch your manners, Bryan, or you'll not be dining with us again."

As her young brother scowled at her, she turned around to look for the butler, then gave a sigh of relief and said, "Ah, there you are, Rivers. We'll put the colonel at the head of the table, and I'll take the foot, and you can lay a fresh place for Lord Pelham between Lady Ramsbottom and Lady Pelham, if you please."

By the time the colonel came downstairs, everything was in order and Sarah made the introductions before he took his place at the table. Robert immediately raised his glass and proposed a toast to the new earl, who did not miss the expression of sadness that came over his hostess's face. But he was pleased to see that she drank to his health with the rest of them.

For Sarah it was a most difficult meal. Although it had been quickly concealed, she had noticed the look of surprise on the colonel's face when he saw how many people were dining at the table. There were so many things she needed to explain to him. That would have to wait until they were finished and she could get him on his own, however, for though conversation at the table was informal as usual, she was just too far away to say anything at all to him without shouting. Perhaps she and Robert could have a few words in private with him afterward, and make sure he did not feel that she and her family had been taking advantage of his absence.

Unlike the earl's, her appetite was sadly lacking, and to her the excellent meal tasted no better than sawdust. Her family appeared to be asking the earl endless questions, particularly young Bryan, but their voices seemed too far away and the brief snatches of conversation she heard made little sense. But at last the meal was over and Rivers was asking if the two gentlemen would like their port served in the dining room or in the library.

"You may serve it in the library, Rivers," Sarah put in quickly, "and you may take my tea in there also. I will join the ladies later."

Her brother's eyebrows rose, but he said nothing as he offered his arm to his sister, and when Rivers had closed the library door behind them, Jethro gave her a questioning look.

"A departure from the usual, my lord," Sarah said, a little flustered, "but I felt some explanation was necessary before you reached any hasty conclusions. At my request, my brother came here to help me keep the estates in order after my husband's death. My stepmama, who brought us up from children, felt she should be with me at this time but could not leave our half-brother and -sister alone. They are not staying in the manor, but at the priory, which is the dower house some distance from here, to which I shall be retiring.

"They have been eating dinner here each night because the priory is sadly lacking in servants, and the kitchen staff here had little to do," she explained, sounding apologetic, "but I will, of course, make more suitable arrangements for tomorrow."

Jethro's lazy smile was infectious. "No explanation is necessary, my lady," he said gently. "I would not have wished you to be alone at such a sorrowful time."

"You've very kind, sir," Sarah said quickly, "but I will be moving to the priory tonight, for it would not be at all the thing for me to stay here now that you are in residence."

"There is something else you should know, Jethro," Robert added, glancing at his sister, who inclined her head in consent. "Mr. Musgrave means to speak to you about a matter your cousin quite obviously overlooked in his will."

Jethro's bushy black eyebrows rose a fraction, and he waited for Robert to explain himself.

"He apparently did not think to set aside any specific funds for my sister's use in the event she was childless, and Mr. Musgrave, who is quite old, did not notice the omission until it was too late." Robert paused when he saw Jethro's puzzled frown, and tried to explain how it came about. "You see, Percy was comparatively young, in excellent health, and had little doubt that he would eventually have sons to inherit his lands and title. He did allocate a most generous allowance for Sarah, as co-guardian of his offspring, and you, by the way, were to have been their other guardian."

"You are quite sure this omission was not my cousin's intent, are you not?" Jethro asked thoughtfully. It seemed inconceivable that such an important matter as a jointure could have been overlooked, and Jethro had no intention of allowing a charming brother and sister to bamboozle him. "There had been no marital discord or quarrel, perhaps, just before the will was penned, that might account for it?"

Sarah had been deceived by the colonel's charm and could not at first believe what she was hearing, but then she became furious and there was a distinct flash of gold in her angry gray eyes.

"Allow me to enlighten you, sir," she snapped. "Percy was the kindest, dearest gentleman that I have ever met, and in the eighteen months we were married, we never had a single angry word. Should you care to stoop so low as to question the servants in this regard, please do so, for I can assure you it will only serve to confirm what I have said.''

She fumbled for a kerchief, then jumped up quickly and was out the door before either gentleman, taken unawares, could do more than rise to his feet.

Jethro looked a little bewildered, for though there was no doubt that he had been testing, he had spoken quietly, as if seeking some simple explanation. ''I had no wish to cause your sister discomfort, Robert, but I merely sought to better understand the reason for the omission. Is she usually so impetuous?'' he asked.

Her brother shook his head and resumed his seat. ''I know she used to have quite a temper, but I haven't seen it in years,'' he admitted. ''However, she's not quite herself at the moment, for despite the difference in their ages, she did think a great deal of Percy, and his death came as a terrible shock to her. Then, having the family descend upon her when what she needed was peace and quiet seems to have got on her nerves somewhat, but there's no gainsaying Lady Pelham when she makes up her mind to do something. That's probably why Sarah's been looking decidedly under the weather these last few days.''

''I think you'd best go after her, Robert, and explain, if you can, that it was never my intention to imply that her marriage was not a normally happy one.'' Jethro looked quite genuinely distressed. ''This was probably not the best time to discuss the matter, for when I'm bone weary I'm inclined to speak before I think. I decided to bypass London and come here directly, so I have been on horseback much of the day. Perhaps you could join me for breakfast in the morning around eight o'clock. After a good night's sleep and a hearty breakfast, this whole thing will look completely different, I'm sure.''

Robert readily agreed, for he did not wish his sister to walk back to the priory alone at night, and in the state she was in when she hurried out, she would probably have preferred to do so than join the others.

Left alone in the handsome oak-paneled library, Jethro put a small log on the fire and watched it start to blaze, then poured himself another glass of port, sat back in the comfortable brown leather armchair, and began to wonder what his ancestors, the men who had sat here before him, had been like. Unless the place was severely encumbered, he was now a very wealthy man, but coming into it this way did not seem quite real—or quite right.

The portrait of Percy in the drawing room was so lifelike that he almost felt that his cousin was still here and might come through the door at any minute and ask what he was doing sitting in his chair and dreaming about his lady wife, for that's what he had caught himself doing several times since she had so hurriedly left the room.

He could certainly understand why Percy had married her. She was quite lovely, but in the Season in London there were always young women more beautiful. Few of them, however, possessed that indefinable quality that mattered so much more.

There was a knock on the door and Rivers came in. "Will there be anything else this evening, milord?" he asked.

Jethro shook his head, suddenly feeling quite exhausted. "Did my batman arrive yet?" he asked, and when Rivers shook his head, he nodded. "Then ask someone, perhaps the late earl's man, to set some water to heat so that I may enjoy the rare luxury of a bath before I get into that inviting bed I glimpsed a little earlier."

Rivers' face showed a rare smile. "I believe water is being kept hot for you, milord, so I'll wish you a good-night."

They were certainly well-trained servants, and anxious to please, Jethro thought, before draining his glass. Then he rose to his feet and went upstairs to a comfort he had not known since he had bought his commission five years before and gone off to fight Napoleon.

* * *

In the small book room of the priory, Lord Robert Pelham was pacing back and forth as he tried quite unsuccessfully to make his sister see reason.

"It was your own fault for trying to discuss matters that should have been left until the morning," he told Sarah. "He was quite obviously exhausted after his journey, for he told me that he'd been on horseback most of the day, having decided not to delay his arrival by spending the night in London."

"I don't care what you say, Rob, he'd no right to imply that my husband had a reason for not wishing to make me an allowance," Sarah said angrily. "It would have been best if he had stayed in town and discussed the matter with the solicitor who drew up the will. Mr. Musgrave knew that Percy never even considered he might die before we had children."

They had been arguing ever since Robert had caught up with her on the narrow road leading to the priory and given her a sound scold for starting out in the darkness alone. The carriage the older ladies always used to go back and forth between the two houses had passed them long ago, and its occupants were already abed by the time Sarah and Robert reached the house. Not yet finished with their argument, they had gone directly to the book room at the back of the priory so as not to disturb the household.

"I'm having breakfast with Jethro at eight in the morning," Robert informed her. "He wants to go over the will and then get some idea of the extent and condition of the estate."

"Does he, indeed?" Sarah looked sharply at her brother. "I was the one left in charge, and you came here only because I asked you to help me, so he can discuss the extent and condition with me also. I'll be downstairs by a quarter to eight in the morning, and we'll go together to the manor."

Robert sighed heavily. "You're adopting a completely contrary attitude about this whole thing, Sarah, and you'll be sorry if you get off on the wrong foot with him, I promise. I know what really happened. You felt guilty because the whole family was there at his dining table, eating his food, when he arrived. Though he did look surprised, he didn't complain, but you were embarrassed, and so anxious to explain that you brought up matters that should have waited until he'd had his port and a good night's rest.''

Sarah looked decidedly indignant. ''I wasn't the one who brought up the matter of the will and the lack of a jointure,'' she protested. ''It was you who decided to talk to him about it. There is just one thing you need to know, you said, and started to tell him about the meeting with Mr. Musgrave. All I went into the library for was to explain about my family and that I would be moving out of the manor tonight.''

Heaving a sigh, Robert got to his feet. ''As usual, you're quite right. Let's go to bed now, and perhaps the whole thing will seem much better after a night's sleep. I'll wait for you in here in the morning, and unless it's raining, we'll walk over to the manor and talk about it on the way.''

She stood up and he slipped a comforting arm around her shoulders; then they went quietly up the back stairs and to the chamber that had hurriedly been prepared for her. Giving her a brotherly hug, he opened the door and pushed her into the waiting arms of her abigail, Betty.

But the following morning he had started to pace the floor impatiently when she had not come down at the time she had specified. It was fortunate that he had ordered the carriage and that it was already at the door, for he had no wish to be late for his first meeting with the new earl.

When he heard her coming down the stairs, he hurried forward to take her arm and assist her into the carriage, and was just about to rip up at her for causing him to be late when he noticed how pale she looked.

''I say, Sarah, you don't look exactly in the pink this morning. Are you coming down with something?'' he asked, frowning.

She shook her head. ''I'm all right, but I'll go through to the kitchen before I leave the manor and have a word with

Cook. Something I ate last night must have upset my stomach, and I want to be sure she's not keeping things too long.''

Robert shrugged. "I had no problem, but then, you've always said I have a cast-iron stomach. You must have needed some fresh air, for you're starting to look much better now.''

She managed a grin, for he had been looking out of the window when she had determinedly pinched her cheeks to give herself a little color. But the air had also been beneficial, and by the time they reached the manor she felt almost back to normal.

Jethro was coming down the stairs as they entered the hall, and there was just time enough for Rivers to add another place setting before the three of them went into the sunny breakfast room.

"How refreshing to find a young lady who rises before noon,'' Jethro remarked with a smile as he held the chair next to his to seat her. "May I help you to some kippers and some eggs, or would you prefer the bacon?''

Sarah murmured, "Just a little toast and eggs to start with, I think, and I'll help myself to some tea.'' She flashed a warning glance at her brother, who looked as if he was going to say something about her; then she took a sip of the tea.

"Did you enjoy a good night's sleep after your long journey?'' she asked politely as Jethro placed a plate of food in front of her.

"Wonderful,'' he told her. "You can have no idea what a feather bed feels like after so many years of sleeping on anything from straw mattresses to hard-packed earth.''

He thought she looked a little pale, but decided to be diplomatic and say nothing, for it was possible that she had not slept very well in a strange bedchamber. One thing he did not wish to do was to antagonize her again if he could help it, for he would much rather make a friend of her than an enemy.

"Did your batman finally get here?" Robert asked, for the new earl was no longer in uniform but wore the well-cut breeches and jacket of a country gentleman.

Jethro nodded, grinning. "Not long after you left, as a matter of fact. He was not in the best of humors, for he'd been wandering around the countryside, quite lost. This place is not easy for a stranger to find after dark."

The two men made a quite hearty breakfast, to Sarah's disgust, and when they were finished, they all adjourned to the library.

3

As soon as they entered the library, Robert went over to the large desk, withdrew a document from the top drawer, then waited until Jethro had seated his sister comfortably in one of the large chairs beside the fire. The new earl's attitude today was nothing if not gently courteous, and Sarah was grateful, because today she wanted no further discord.

As Jethro took the chair across from her, Robert handed him a copy of the will, then stood nearby to answer any questions the earl might pose, for he was most certainly giving it very careful perusal.

Finally Jethro looked up. "I see what you mean," he said at last, "for Percy clearly had thought only as far ahead as he felt necessary at the time this was written. I cannot help but wonder, however, why the solicitor did not point out the need to make arrangements for certain possible contingencies. It was most decidedly his place to do so."

"You will understand, I am sure, when you meet Mr. Musgrave, for he is getting on in years," Robert said with a slight shrug. "He probably thought that he'd be dead and buried long before Percy would, and that a younger partner would then take over and suggest a new will if it should be necessary."

Jethro nodded thoughtfully, then turned to Sarah. "Please forgive my thoughtless questions of last evening, my lady. It was never my intention to cause you pain, but simply to better understand the situation."

She inclined her head and smiled faintly, reluctant to acquit him of all blame until she heard his recommendations.

"There's no question that some provision has to be made for you, but I am a little at a loss, for I have never before had anything to do with a matter of this sort. Quite frankly, having been out of the country for a number of years and out of touch with present-day costs, I have not the slightest idea of what might constitute a generous or a miserly amount to set aside." He smiled apologetically, and Sarah found herself smiling back. "I'll send Mr. Musgrave a note and request that he come here again, at his first convenience, but in the meantime I must be sure that you are as comfortable as possible at the priory, which I have not as yet seen.

"It would seem the simplest thing for now if some of the servants from the manor were to go to work for you there. If their quarters at the priory are not large enough, some of them could continue to sleep here, and then when your family departs, you could send back the ones for whom you have no further need. Does that sound sensible to you, my lady?"

Sarah thought it an ideal arrangement, but there was also another question to settle.

"Most sensible, sir," she said quietly. "I did request that for the time being Mrs. Pennyfarthing order supplies for the priory when she buys for here, but keep a separate reckoning, of course. I trust that this meets with your approval, my lord?"

"Of course," Jethro readily agreed, "but only if I can persuade you to discontinue so much formality and allow me to call you Cousin Sarah while you call me Cousin Jethro. How does that sound?"

"To me it makes a lot of sense," Robert said with a grin. "But then, it was never my problem."

Sarah suddenly felt better than she had felt all morning.

Robert was right: it had been foolish to try to talk about such matters last night when she was on edge and Cousin Jethro was travel-weary. Because of her brother's generous help, the affairs of the estate were in excellent order, and she knew that the rest of the morning was bound to go smoothly. Rather than stay for the business discussion, she would go and talk to Mrs. Pennyfarthing now about moving some additional staff over to the priory.

But just as she was about to excuse herself, she heard a commotion in the hall, and then the door swung open and Bryan came running in, closely followed by one of the footmen.

Robert, who had been setting the various papers and ledgers on the desk, turned around just in time to grab hold of his half-brother while the snarling footman came to a halt nearby.

"Pray, what is the meaning of this?" Jethro asked, giving the footman an icy stare. "Your name?"

"Grimsby, milord, an' I'm sorry to disturb you, but I'd no idea there was anyone in 'ere. The young varmint pocketed my fishin' lures an' made off with 'em."

"Do you have something belonging to this person, Bryan?" Jethro asked quietly.

"No, I don't, sir, for they're not his at all," Bryan said defiantly. "I found them in the attic here, and Sarah said I might use them."

"Has the footman been teaching you to fish?" Sarah asked.

Bryan turned to face his sister. "He said he would, Sarah, but he hasn't shown me anything yet. He just took the rods and lures from me and then said he'd lost them. I found them in his room, but then I heard him coming, so I grabbed the lures and ran."

"So you stole my property, Grimsby, did you?" Jethro suggested, a threatening note in his voice. The footman's face turned white, for such a charge was serious indeed.

" 'E's lyin', milord," he whined. "I never said I'd lost 'em. I was just keepin' 'em in my room until me day off, when I was goin' to teach 'im 'ow to use 'em. 'E's a regular little liar, that one. You can't believe a word 'e says.''

"That's not true. I don't tell lies,'' Bryan said furiously.

Jethro looked at Sarah and raised his eyebrows in question.

"I'm sure I heard this person say at first that the lures were his property, when, of course, they were not. Bryan's a little monkey and full of mischief, but one thing I've never known him to do is lie. Isn't that so, Robert?'' she asked.

Her brother nodded, but did not relax his hold on the youngster.

"How long have you worked here?'' Jethro asked the footman.

"Six months, milord,'' the man said, then added, as if realizing it to be a short time, "but I used to work for the old master before 'is wife died.''

"Then I believe you have worked here long enough,'' Jethro said. "Pack your things and be out of here within the hour. And do not take anything with you that does not belong to you or, I assure you, you will regret it.''

As the scowling footman hurried out of the room, Jethro turned to Bryan.

"And as for you, young man, if you have any problem with the staff here, come to me. You're not big enough to handle it yourself, and certainly not by going into other people's bedchambers. When Grimsby has left the premises, you may collect those rods and set them aside. If you really want to learn to fish, you need not ask servants, I'll teach you myself.'' He saw the look of delight in the boy's eyes, but added sternly, "And in the future, if you are told not to disturb me, and you still do so, I will deal with you personally. Now, off with you, for we have work to do.''

Bryan did not need to be told twice. He was across the room in a flash, and Sarah concentrated her attention upon the design of the carpet as she waited to hear the heavy door slam, as usual, behind him, but for once he remembered to close it quietly.

"Now that I have committed myself, I hope there is a nearby stream," Jethro remarked with a grin.

Sarah chuckled with relief. "There's an excellent trout stream where Percy apparently spent many happy hours in his youth," she told him. "I do hope you realize that Bryan will hold you to it, for he is most anxious to learn."

"I never make promises I don't keep," Jethro said, and there was a look in his eyes as he gazed directly into Sarah's that gave her the most extraordinary feeling of breathlessness. It was only with the greatest effort that she was able to break the spell and lower her eyes to a spot on the carpet.

"I think I'll leave you gentlemen to those ledgers and seek out Mrs. Pennyfarthing, for there's much to be done before nightfall if the priory is to be made more comfortable," she said, rising, then added as both gentlemen sprang to their feet, "Please sit down, for I've grown quite accustomed to opening doors for myself."

"I sent the carriage back, in case the ladies had plans to go out," Robert said as he escorted her to the door that Jethro held open. "If you don't feel like walking when you're finished here, don't start out, but call for the other carriage."

Jethro closed the door behind Sarah and then the two men went over to the desk, Robert pulling up another chair so that he could explain details to Jethro as they went along, but the latter looked at him with an expression of concern on his face. "Is your sister not feeling well?" he asked. "Do you think you should perhaps have taken her back?"

Robert shook his head. "No, she's fine. Sarah's always been as healthy as a horse, but she may have eaten something last night that didn't agree with her. She means to talk to Cook before she goes back to be sure that the meats and things are being stored properly. Sometimes the servants get lax when the mistress of the house is as busy as she's been lately."

Jethro nodded, satisfied with the explanation, and soon became immersed in the day-to-day problems of an estate that was considerably larger than anything he had ever dreamed of owning. When there was a knock on the door and Rivers came in to inquire if they were ready for luncheon, both gentlemen were amazed that it was so late.

"I thought that perhaps you would like to take a ride over part of the property this afternoon, meet some of the people we've spoken about, and get the feel of things," Robert suggested as they ate mutton pie washed down with a tankard of home-brewed ale.

"It sounds like a splendid idea," Jethro agreed. "I much prefer to see things for myself than to study all this book work, but I can't thank you enough for keeping the records in such good order. To be honest, I expected to find everything in quite a muddle, and dreaded having to sort it all out, for I clearly recall what a mess my own father inherited when Grandpapa passed on."

"You should thank my sister for most of it, for she's got an aptitude for figures and took care of nearly everything we saw this morning. She asked my help only because she was unfamiliar with the actual work going on and knew only the bailiff and a few of the others Percy had relied upon." Robert chuckled. "She's got a good head on her shoulders, but sometimes lets her temper get the better of her. She was furious last night when you had excluded her from our meeting today."

"Really?" Jethro said, dryly. "I would never have believed it from the charming way in which she left us last evening."

Robert grinned, then turned toward the door.

Orders had already been given for their horses to be brought around, and they set off at a steady trot to the first of the numerous small tenant farms.

Sarah saw them start out as she glanced out of the window of a room at the back of the house that she had made into her own private sitting room/study when she first came to the manor. It was one of the places she would miss from now on, and she wished she might still use it, for with her family firmly established at the priory there was little privacy there. She wondered if Cousin Jethro realized just how difficult it would be to persuade her stepmama to return to her own home.

She had sent for Mrs. Pennyfarthing, and a few minutes later the motherly housekeeper knocked on the door and came bustling in, followed by a maid with a simple meal set on a tray.

"I heard that you had not yet had luncheon, milady," the housekeeper said, "and thought you might like to have a little something while we talk."

"That was very thoughtful of you, and as a matter of fact, I had just begun to feel hungry. Won't you join me?" Sarah asked.

"I'll not say no to a cup of tea," the older woman admitted, "but I had a bite to eat more than an hour ago. Did you get a chance to talk to the new earl about what's to be done at the priory?"

Sarah nodded and started to explain what she had in mind, and before long they had a workable plan for staff to look after both houses. She carefully kept the needs of the priory to a minimum, for she dared not let Lady Pelham become too comfortable.

"Mrs. Carter is a very good plain cook," the housekeeper said, in complete agreement with her ladyship's choice for the priory, "and I think it might be best if pastries and cakes were made here and sent over to the priory as you need them, don't you?"

"Yes, but let's not overdo, for Lord Pelham rarely partakes of sweets and pastries," Sarah warned. "I think a cake and a few biscuits for tea, and a sweet for after dinner each day will suffice. My sister does not eat very much for fear of becoming fat, but we'll have to keep young Bryan out of the kitchen if we want anything left."

"Are you sure that will be enough, milady? I've noticed that Lady Pelham has quite a sweet tooth," the housekeeper observed.

Sarah smiled. "I would not wish to be accused of causing my stepmama's gowns to be let out," she said with a twinkle in her eyes. "She finds it difficult to resist such tempting treats. It would be a different matter could she be persuaded to walk a little more, speaking of which, it's time I started back for the priory, or the servants will be there before me and standing around waiting for instructions."

She left then, and did not call for a carriage but set out at such a brisk pace along the side of the private road that by the time she reached the priory she was a little out of breath and had to stand for a moment in the hall before joining Lady Pelham and her aunt in the drawing room.

The door was open and she could hear the two ladies conversing and see reflected in the mirror the well-made but rather plain furniture, which she happened to like, but which Adele found most distasteful.

"I do hope you came to some satisfactory arrangement for staffing this place, Sarah," Lady Pelham began as soon as she saw her stepdaughter. "I'm sure your late husband would not have wished you to live in this way. Why, at luncheon today there was only one footman to attend us. And you really must insist on hiring a butler, or all the riffraff of the neighborhood will be let in on the pretext of offering condolences."

"I'm afraid that I'm not in a position to insist upon anything at the moment, Adele," Sarah said dryly. "However, the earl has been most kind in lending me a number of staff from the manor, and henceforth we should be able to go along with a minimum of discomfort. If they are not yet already in the kitchen awaiting instructions, they will be here very shortly."

Somewhat mollified, Lady Pelham asked, "Has Jethro agreed to give you the portion Percy overlooked, then?"

"Nothing can be decided until the earl sees Mr. Musgrave," Sarah said quietly, "but in the meantime we can hardly say we are living like paupers here. There are already more servants employed here than you have at home, Adele.''

"But your papa was not so well-placed as Percy, and Robert insists that he must put monies back into the land instead of keeping up the standard of living I was always accustomed to," Lady Pelham said testily. "I must have an abigail, for that girl of yours is never there when I want anything doing. And she's a little too pert for my liking too."

"Now, Adele," Lady Agatha Ramsbottom said sharply, "the girl has enough to do looking after my niece without trying to help the pair of us. You should have brought your own girl with you."

Sarah was very fond of the old lady, who so seldom interfered, and she gave her a warm smile of thanks for her support, though she knew that Adele would not be at all pleased.

"I should have done so if you had not decided to come with us, Agatha," Adele snaped, "but you know quite well that there was no room inside the carriage for another person."

"If she was not so hoity-toity, she could have ridden on the box with the coachman," the older lady retorted. "In my day only governesses rode inside with the family."

As this was an old argument likely to go on for some time, Sarah slipped quietly out of the room and went in search of the additional servants from the manor. They were, as she had suspected, all sitting around the kitchen table drinking tea, and they jumped guiltily to their feet when she walked in.

"I'm glad you got here so promptly," she told them, smiling pleasantly, "and I would just like to explain your duties. Mrs. Carter, you will, as I am sure Mrs. Penny-farthing explained, take charge of the kitchen. All meals will be cooked here now except for cakes, pastries, and sweets. These will be brought over every day from the manor. Jennie, you are to assist Lady Pelham and Lady Ramsbottom with their gowns and such, and you, George, will be acting butler here, answering the door and making sure that all meals are served promptly and correctly. Millie and Tom, you are to help wherever you might be needed, and I do not expect to find any of you sitting here drinking tea again at this hour.''

Turning on her heel, she swept out of the room and took the back stairs to her own chamber, a much smaller room than the one she had occupied at the manor, but quite adequate for now. Lady Pelham had taken the largest bed-chamber for herself, but Sarah did not mind, for this one was a little away from the others, toward the back of the house, and it afforded more privacy.

She sank gratefully into the one armchair before the small fireplace and closed her eyes, recalling that she and Robert had stayed up much later than usual last night, which was probably why she was a little tired.

She must have fallen asleep, for she awoke with a start when the door opened and Betty, her abigail, came bustling in.

''I'm sorry, milady, I was ironing some of your things in the laundry room and no one told me you'd come back,'' the girl started to say, then realized she had woken her mistress. ''I am sorry, milady, but it's not like you to be asleep in the middle of the day, is it, now? But then, you were up late last night.''

Sarah shook her head and blinked her eyes, still trying to wake up. ''I must have needed it, for I feel much better now,'' she said, a little surprised. ''I spoke to Cook and she assured me the meat served last night was not off in the slightest, so I don't know what could have upset me.''

She frowned at Betty, for the girl had the oddest expression on her face. ''Why are you looking like that? Do you know what it was that upset my stomach?''

''I think so, milady,'' the girl said. ''Do you recall that you missed your menses when the earl was killed, and we thought it was the shock as did it? Well, it's just over a month since, isn't it?''

Sarah looked incredulous for a moment. Then her face lit

up and she felt like shouting with pure joy, for there was nothing she would like more than to have Percy's child. It was still a little too soon to be sure, though, and she did not want to be too hopeful for fear that she might be bitterly disappointed.

"It is possible, I'll admit, Betty, but you must not say a word to anyone as yet, for we can't be sure, and you know how my stepmama would carry on if she had the slightest idea." The excitement faded from her expressive face and her eyes filled with tears as she murmured, "The earl wanted a child so very much. How sad if he finally created one and never knew it."

Betty put an arm around her mistress's shoulders. "If it's to be, he'll know of it, milady," she said quietly, "for it'll be part of God's plan."

She moved away, and left her mistress staring thoughtfully into the small fire. Then she remembered why she had hurried up the stairs. "It's almost time for tea, milady. Aren't you going to join the others in the drawing room?"

Sarah sighed. "I really don't wish to at all, particularly now, but I suppose I must. I'll not change my gown, but perhaps you could make my hair look a little less untidy. I'm afraid it got quite windblown as I walked back from the manor."

Five minutes later, looking much more rested and at peace than she had earlier in the day, she went slowly down the stairs to join her family.

4

"Good afternoon, Adele, Aunt Agatha," Sarah said with forced cheerfulness as she joined the ladies for tea. "I do hope Jennie proves to be of assistance to you both, for Mrs. Pennyfarthing assured me that she is an excellent needlewoman, has been taught by an older sister to look after a lady's wardrobe, and is most talented at arranging hair."

Lady Pelham frowned. She was in a mood when nothing and no one could please her. "It is always a problem getting properly trained servants in the country, but I've no doubt that by the time we are ready to return north, the girl will be fairly capable."

"At least she appears willing enough, in fact almost eager, Adele," Lady Agatha said, "and I've always found that a little patience with a young girl reaps its own reward."

"If that is a way of telling me that you will be keeping the girl in your chamber half the evening, Agatha, I'd best make sure she comes to me first, or dinner will be finished before I'm dressed and downstairs," Lady Pelham snapped, then turned back to Sarah. "And what have you been doing all day, my dear, now that the new earl is finally here? I understand he's been out with Robert all afternoon."

"I've been arranging the duties of the additional staff for

the priory you were so anxious about,'' Sarah said a little tartly. ''You have presumably met George, one of the senior footmen from the manor, who will serve as butler here for the time being; and Mrs. Carter, who is the second cook at the manor must, at this very moment, be starting to prepare dinner for us here this evening.''

Lady Pelham looked at her stepdaughter rather strangely. ''Do you mean that we are no longer to dine at the manor each evening? Did the new earl decide this?''

''Though I am quite sure he would prefer his privacy, Adele, the decision was mine, for I cannot continue to use the manor as if it were still my home,'' Sarah said sharply. She was about to say more, but was saved by a knock on the door and the entry of George and one of the maids with the tea tray.

Lady Pelham glanced quickly at the tray, on which were arranged thinly sliced bread and butter, strawberry jam, fruitcake slices, ginger biscuits, and orange puffs. Once the door had closed behind the servants, she looked reproachfully at her stepdaughter, then said, ''I assume that the cook did not have time to prepare the kind of tea tray to which I am accustomed, my dear, and that this is not what we are to expect from now onward?''

''Now, Adele, how much more could you want? If we kept town hours it would be different, but you'll be having dinner shortly,'' Sarah protested, though she was unable to help smiling at Lady Pelham's petulant expression. ''And you did complain that your clothes were becoming a trifle too tight.''

''It's a sight more than you serve for tea at your own home, Adele,'' Lady Agatha declared, ''so what are you fretting about? I don't believe in sending most of it back to the kitchen for the servants to eat, though I'll admit that when young Bryan's about, there's never aught but crumbs left.''

With a sniff, Lady Pelham reached for a piece of cake and took the cup of tea Sarah had poured for her. She tasted the cake; then, when she could find nothing more to complain of, she recalled her earlier conversation.

"To get back to dinner," she said to Sarah. "That nice young man seemed more than pleased that we were having dinner up at the manor last night. I believe that we should continue to do so until he indicates that he is averse to such a plan. There is really not enough room for us all to eat in the dining room here, you know."

"There will be tonight," Sarah said firmly, her smile dimming, for she was becoming irritated with her stepmama's constant animadversions, "for extra leaves were put into the dining table this afternoon."

A light tap sounded on the door, and George entered, going over to Sarah and presenting a card on a silver tray.

"Show her in, George, and send for a fresh pot of tea," she told him, then turned to the two ladies. "One of our neighbors is paying a condolence call. I'm sure you will enjoy meeting her."

A moment later Sarah went forward to greet a middle-aged lady of considerable girth and a quite startling appearance. She had a round, jolly face, twinkling blue eyes, and curls of a most unlikely shade of gold that glinted beneath a large unfashionable hat bedecked with flowers, fruit, and feathers. Her bright green pelisse was trimmed down the front and around the hem with black fur.

"Sarah, love," she cried, taking both of Sarah's hands in her own, "I just this minute got back from helping my Josie nurse her sick youngsters through the measles, and heard the dreadful news. To lose such a fine man in the prime of life—I just can't tell you how sorry I am! And for you to have to leave the manor and come to this place is nothing less than a crying shame." She shook her head and the grapes on her hat swung dangerously from side to side for a moment before resuming their position.

Taking advantage of the pause, Sarah stepped to one side and performed the introductions, then offered Mrs. Lofthouse the large wing chair, for she knew from past experience that if her friend once settled down on a couch, it would take several footmen to help her up.

"Do you live in the neighborhood?" Lady Pelham asked politely.

"Just over the hill," Mrs. Lofthouse said, struggling to remove a purple glove. "When Mr. Lofthouse retired, he decided this must be the prettiest spot in the whole of England, so he bought Bedford Grange. And the time I had persuading him not to change the name to Lofthouse Grange, you'd never believe."

The glove was finally off, and she reached out fingers that sparkled with jeweled rings to help herself to a slice of fruitcake.

"Now, Sarah, tell me what the new earl is like. I've heard all about his looks, of course, and that he's a soldier, for half the chits in the area are wondering how they can get to meet him. But is he a good man, like Percy was?" she asked bluntly.

"He's not yet been here more than a day, so I really can't say, Lillian, but my brother, Robert, seems to have taken quite a liking to him. He's with him now, I believe, showing him the extent of the estates." Sarah was not willing to commit herself as yet, for it seemed that he had been both harsh and kind to her, and she had no way of knowing which might be his normal manner. She smiled ruefully. "He is a colonel, of course, and accustomed to giving orders and having them obeyed without question."

"Surely's he's not been ordering you about, has he?" Mrs. Lofthouse sounded highly indignant but she relaxed when Sarah shook her head. "I should think not, for that would be a fine thing indeed, after turning you out of your home."

"He did not ask me to leave, Lillian"—Sarah was anxious not to give the new earl a bad name—"but I had to, for it would not have been at all the thing for me to stay in the manor with him in residence. It would have set the whole neighborhood to gossiping, you must know."

"Their gossip wouldn't worry me for a minute, but I know how it would upset a lady like you," Mrs. Lofthouse said sympathetically, "and I'd not like that to happen, but I don't care to think of you staying alone in this dismal place once your family have gone home.''

"She need not worry about that for the time being,'' Lady Pelham said brusquely, "for we'll not be leaving until she's much more comfortably settled. I couldn't sleep at night if I thought my dear Sarah was unhappy and alone here. In fact, I've been thinking that you should consider hiring a companion, Sarah. It would most certainly give rise to talk if someone as young as you set up housekeeping alone, even though you are a widow.''

"I would hate to have a stranger here just to give me consequence, but was wondering if you might perhaps be able to spare Aunt Agatha to stay on with me, Adele.'' Sarah had only just thought of it, but realized it would be an ideal solution, for it was not so much a matter of whether people talked or not, as the fact that she had really no wish to live completely alone.

Lady Ramsbottom had been sitting quietly listening to the conversation, but taking no part in it, something she tended to do more frequently as Lady Pelham became increasingly voluble. Now, however, her watery blue eyes sparkled, and her wrinkled face, if not actually breaking into a smile, took on an added glow.

"Why not? It would certainly save you having to pay someone else to sit around and do nothing all day,'' Lady Pelham said practically, with her usual want of tact. "And I believe the climate down here would be better for her rheumatism. Would you like to stay with Sarah?'' she asked the older lady, speaking louder and more slowly, as if to a half-wit.

"If she wants me to keep her company, then I'm sure I've no objections,'' Lady Agatha said gruffly, trying not to show how pleased she was with the arrangement, but spoiling it by adding, "If you like, you can send for the rest of my things tomorrow.''

There was a loud commotion in the hall, the sound that always heralded the arrival of young Bryan, and he suddenly burst into the room, stopping short, however, when he saw his sister's guest. His brown hair was still slightly damp from having been hurriedly slicked down, but his boots bore traces of leaf mold from the woods.

Unlike his mama, he quite obviously found Mrs. Lofthouse's appearance most intriguing. He walked over to her at once to introduce himself, and as she had grandsons of about the same age, he was an immediate success.

"If you're a good friend of Sarah's, you must live around here, ma'am," he said matter-of-factly, then asked, "Do you fish the streams?"

Her large frame shook as Mrs. Lofthouse laughed heartily. "Not since I was about your age, young man. If I sat myself down beside a stream these days, they'd never be able to get me up again."

Bryan gave a loud chortle as he pictured her struggles, but Lady Pelham was most decidedly not amused.

"Did you wash your hands before you came in, Bryan? I can tell you did not clean your boots, for they're leaving a mess all over your sister's carpet," she snapped. "Go and have them taken care of before you have your tea."

"He may just as well stay, for the damage is already done, Adele, and the tea will be quite cold by the time he returns," Sarah pleaded.

It was to no avail, however. This was to be one of the rare occasions when Lady Pelham exercised some control over her young son, and he sulkily left the drawing room to seek the aid of one of the servants.

Ten minutes later, when Bryan had still not returned, Mrs. Lofthouse carefully placed her cup and saucer on a nearby table. "I'd best be off, Sarah, for having been away so long, there's much to be done. Just you remember, if there's anything at all I can do to help, you only have to send word and I'll be here before you know it."

She managed to get out of the chair without aid, though her hat became slightly askew in the struggle, and without even bothering to glance in a mirror, she tugged it back into place. Then she stood for a moment drawing on her gloves and looking at Lady Pelham as she did so, with a half-smile on her face.

"It was a pleasure, my lady," she said, "and I wish you a safe journey home. That's a fine, spunky youngster you have there, and I enjoyed meeting him. Lady Ramsbottom, when you're settled in, have Sarah bring you over to Bedford Grange and have tea with us."

"I'll see you out, Lillian," Sarah said, leading the way and closing the door firmly behind her.

"What a dreadfully vulgar woman," Lady Pelham remarked with an expression of distaste on her face, carefully keeping her voice low in case it could be heard in the hall. "I shall regard it your duty after we leave, Agatha, to discourage Sarah from having any further communication with such an encroaching creature. It cannot but do harm to Sarah's standing in the neighborhood to entertain a woman of that sort, and I'm most surprised at Percy for permitting it."

Lady Agatha gave her the blank, questioning look she had carefully practiced over the past few years, which Lady Pelham had incorrectly assumed to mean that she had grown a little hard of hearing. On this occasion, as a raised voice might have carried into the hall, the latter was forced to await a more opportune moment to repeat her instruction. Her stepdaughter would be returning at any moment, she felt sure, and she could then make quite clear her views about the inadvisability of having anything more to do with such a woman.

She waited in vain, however, for Sarah, having finished her own tea, went directly to the kitchen to make sure that Bryan's schoolboy appetite was being appeased.

She found him sitting at the kitchen table absorbed in an experiment to see just how much strawberry jam would fit onto one piece of bread and butter. He looked up and grinned at her before carefully sliding the whole piece into his mouth at once.

"I don't know where you put so much food," she told him. "You must have a hollow leg that it all goes into."

"You mean the wooden kind that you can just screw off? I'm not sure I'd like that very much, 'cause it would make too much noise and I couldn't creep up on people," he decided.

Sarah pointed a warning finger at him. "I'm glad you mentioned it, for you've reminded me that I meant to have a word with you on that very subject. I don't know what you hope to learn by listening outside doors, young man, but one of these days you'll hear something you wish you hadn't," she scolded.

"Who told you I listen at doors? I'll bet it was old Rivers, for he's just mad at me 'cause I can hear more than he can," Bryan asserted, not realizing he had just admitted to the offense.

"If he catches you and takes you to the earl, there'll be no fishing lessons, you know," Sarah warned. "It's a very sneaky thing to do, and most people intensely dislike being spied upon."

She watched his expressive young face, knowing quite well that the possible loss of fishing lessons was the far more effective deterrent.

Bryan sighed and looked a little sheepish. "All right, but it's the only way I can find out what's going on, for nobody ever tells me anything 'cept what I should and shouldn't do," he protested, pulling a face. Then he suddenly grinned. "He's going to teach me after tea tomorrow. I saw him with Robert this afternoon, and he said that's the time the fish bite."

Sarah was suddenly unaccountably pleased with Jethro. He must be extremely busy trying to learn everything at once, yet he had not forgotten the promise he had made to the youngster. Perhaps she would take a stroll down to the stream tomorrow, after tea, and see how they went along.

As Bryan finished his tea and ran out of the kitchen, she crossed the room to see how preparations for tonight's dinner were progressing. Because it was the first they'd had in the priory, and also because she knew Adele would complain at the least thing, she particularly wanted it to be a success. She had ordered a tureen of turtle removed with fish, and this was in turn removed with a rib of beef. There were to be side dishes of veal cutlets and braised ham, a quantity of vegetables, and then several creams, jellies, and cakes.

Mrs. Carter gave a little bob when Sarah approached, then continued with her work. She appeared to be a methodical woman, for preparations were obviously well in hand, so Sarah went next to the dining room. This was, however, a mistake, for Lady Pelham was there before her, inspecting the china in the large cabinet and looking critically at the dining table.

"If there is anything I do dislike, it's to sit too close at table," Lady Pelham pronounced, a distasteful expression on her face. "I believe you're making a mistake you will regret, Sarah, for I'm sure the earl would welcome company at dinner. He certainly appeared to enjoy himself last evening. But there's no gainsaying you once you get your mind set on something. You've been that way for as long as I've known you."

"There's ample room at that table for eight or ten people," Sarah said quietly, "but I am aware that the size of the table is not the problem."

"If you had only been a little more pleasant to the new earl, he would have invited us to dine at the manor every evening," Lady Pelham snapped. "But you needs must quarrel with him the minute he arrived and so we're forced to eat our meal each evening in a dining room that is no bigger than a maid's bedchamber."

Not for the first time, Sarah wished that her stepmama had not come with Rob, "to bear her company in her time of sorrow," as she had put it, for her presence had considerably added to her problems. But even if the earl had suggested they continue to dine at the manor, she would have been obliged to decline, for there would then have been no knowing how much longer Lady Pelham would stay here. This constant grumbling was, however, driving her to distraction.

She tried once more to make her stepmama understand. "The manor has been my home for the past eighteen months, Adele. You quite obviously have no idea how much I dislike having to give it up and move into a place that I've always loathed and detested. But I simply could not continue to dine there as a guest, no matter how much you preferred that we do so."

Lady Pelham either would not or could not understand, however. "When you know how much more comfortable we would all be there, I think you might have at least endeavored to accept your changed status," she remarked. "How will you go along when he marries and brings in a new countess to rule the household?"

"By the time that happens, Sarah will be much more able to cope with her loss, Adele. I believe you forget that you came here to be of help, not to make things more difficult for her to bear."

Lady Pelham swung around, for she had not heard Robert enter the room.

"I know it's almost time for us to dress for dinner, and I need to have a word with Sarah before I go up, so if you will excuse us, Adele . . ." he added quietly.

He waited until Lady Pelham left and he had closed the door behind her before turning and putting an arm around his sister's shoulders. "Now I can fully understand why you wished that I had not brought her with me. Have you any idea how much longer she means to remain here?"

She shook her head. "At least a fortnight, I imagine. It was decided today that Aunt Agatha will not go back, but will stay here with me. I had no great wish for a companion, but neither did I want to live in this place alone, and if you'd seen her face when I suggested that she remain here, you'd have been as pleased as I am with the arrangement."

"I'm afraid I have been almost as lacking in perception as Adele, for I had never given a thought to how you felt about leaving the manor—or how much you hated this place," he told her quietly. "Do you think you may grow to like it better once you've settled in and made some changes?"

She shook her head. "I know I'm being ridiculous, but eighteen months is not long to grow so attached to a place like the manor, but I only needed to see the priory once to dislike it," she said ruefully. "But I would not want to dine with Jethro every evening anyway, for I'm not sure that I like him very much. I've never cared for military gentlemen, for they have always seemed too domineering for me."

"You're probably just upset about everything right now, and it's only to be expected. So far as I can see, though, he's not at all domineering, but most agreeable and easy to get along with," he told her. "It's possibly his size that bothers you, for he is large, and all muscle, from what I can see."

She sighed. "I know I'm being a grouch, and I don't even like my own company at the moment. The worst thing is, though, that I find myself becoming furious with Percy for taking that ridiculous jump and thus putting me in a position where I must depend upon a complete stranger's generosity for the very food I eat and the clothes I put on my back. It's so demeaning, Rob."

"Please stop worrying about it," he said, giving her a gentle shake. "I've always believed that things have a way of working out, if you'll only let them. Now, tell me what you've planned for dinner tonight, for I have a feeling it's going to be something quite special."

She listed all the items she had ordered, most of which were his favorites, and then left him to go and change her gown and put on yet another black one. Meanwhile, he went down into the cellars, for he knew that Jethro had given orders for most of the wines in the cellars of the manor to be transferrred here. When he had explained that he felt they belonged to Sarah, Robert had wanted to ask him to dine with them, but thought he'd best wait awhile before making the suggestion.

5

" "Perhaps this won't keep on for long, milady. I
remember when my sister, Clara, had her first, it
lasted only a month or so and then she felt better than she'd
ever felt before in her life." Betty eyed her mistress
sympathetically.

"But at least she didn't have to try to hide it from everyone
until her stepmama left. I believe that after a month or more
of this, I'll be like a wet rag—and someone is bound to realize
what is wrong soon, for I was asked several times yesterday
if I was coming down with something. Is there nothing I can
take to stop it? It's not yet eight o'clock and I feel as tired
as if I'd never slept," she grumbled.

"Here, take a drink of this fresh tea, and then let's see
if you can get a dry biscuit down. I've heard that it helps,"
Betty said coaxingly.

Sarah sipped the tea, and remembered something. "You'd
best make sure that the door is locked, Betty, for I'd not like
my stepmama to come walking in and see me like this."

She nibbled on the biscuit, which tasted quite good except
for the lack of butter, but Betty had assured her that it must
be eaten dry. To her surprise, she started to feel a little better
almost at once.

"I don't know where you got these from, but you'd best

53

make sure that we have plenty, for it seems that you're right and I'll be needing them each morning for some time. At least I don't believe I look as bad as I did yesterday.''

"You look fine, milady," Betty assured her. "And if you're a bit pale, I can always give you a bit of color out of a pot."

"My stepmama would think I've really become depraved if she knew I was using paint and powder," Sarah said with a chuckle. Then she got up from the chair and took a close look at her face. She pinched her cheeks to bring a little flush to them, then stepped back and allowed Betty to help her on with a fresh black gown.

"I think it might be as well to forgo breakfast for the moment. I'll take a walk up to the manor first, and make sure everything is going along all right there," she decided, for the fresh air helped, as a rule. "It's almost a week since the earl arrived, and I expect I'll find that quite a few changes have been made."

"If you ask me," Betty said, "it's about time. I was never so glad to see anything as when you had them clean the old place from top to bottom. Mrs. Pennyfarthing was saying only the other day that she doesn't remember when it looked and smelled so fresh before. But don't you go overdoing it, milady, and don't miss breakfast altogether, for this is no time to starve yourself."

Sarah was smiling as she left the house. She wondered what she would have done these last few weeks since her stepmama arrived if it had not been for Betty's gruff kindness. There were times when the maid went too far, but it was only because she wanted the best for her, and it was a relief that she knew how to keep a still tongue in her head.

The morning was brisk, but she had stout boots on her feet and a warm shawl around her shoulders, and she started out at a good pace along the carriage road. She did not expect to meet anyone at this hour, so it came as a surprise to notice, as she neared the manor, the small figure standing behind a cluster of trees, watching the front door.

She recognized her young half-sister at once, but could not think of any reason for her strange behavior. To the best of her knowledge, Meg was, and always had been, a slugabed, and as she had seldom seen her down early for breakfast, she has assumed that the girl had little to do and liked to sleep late.

Sarah would have stopped to talk with her and find out why she was out so early, but as she drew closer, Meg disappeared into the nearby woods, and by the time Sarah had reached the spot where her sister had been standing, there was no one in sight.

Taking the path toward the rear of the house, she entered through the back door and went directly in search of the housekeeper.

It did not take long for her to find Mrs. Pennyfarthing, for Cook had just seen her going toward the pantries. A few minutes later Sarah was being fussed over like a lost chick and then taken to the housekeeper's sitting room for a bite of breakfast and a good coz.

"How lovely you look this morning, milady. The walk must have done you good and put roses in your cheeks and a sparkle in your eyes. How long is Lady Pelham staying? I'd have thought, by now, that she'd have been anxious to get back to where she comes from and see that everything is going along all right there." She beamed at Sarah, her round, motherly face expressing so much pleasure at her visit that Sarah could not help but feel glad she had come.

"I really don't know," she admitted. "She's probably enjoying being away from her many duties, particularly as Bryan has been very much better behaved since the earl started paying him so much attention. And I must say that the trout have been a delicious addition to the dinner menu. How is everything going along here?"

"Oh, he's an easy master, milady. He must have had such a hard life on the Peninsula that he is a little too easy to please, and it's mine and Rivers' opinion that we shall have to keep the staff on their toes, for he is much too kindhearted for his own good.'' Mrs. Pennyfarthing shook her head. ''You might think, him being a colonel, that he'd be used to ordering people around, but he doesn't seem to want to.''

Sarah nodded, though she did not quite agree with the housekeeper's conclusion. It was more likely that he was so busy trying to learn everything as quickly as possible that he could not be bothered calling the staff to task for minor infringements.

''Did you wish to speak with him, milady?'' the house-keeper asked. ''If you do, you'd best catch him before he leaves the breakfast room, for he makes an early start and will be away the minute he's finished eating.''

Shaking her head, Sarah said, ''It was such a lovely morning that I couldn't resist taking a walk, and I chose this direction so that I might visit with you for a while.'' She tried to sound casual as she went on, ''I was surprised to see my sister in the distance. Does she come over here often?''

Mrs. Pennyfarthing gave her a sharp glance. ''I was wondering when one of you would notice,'' she said. ''It seems as if she's taken a fancy to the earl, and she hangs about outside the stables to catch a glimpse of him almost every day. It's harmless enough, I'm sure, and he hasn't seemed to notice yet, but you might perhaps want to have a word with her or her mother.''

''Oh, dear.'' Sarah sat frowning for a moment. ''I don't really think I want to, but would much rather leave it to her mama. I'm sure I do not recall ever feeling that way myself, and I simply would not know what to say to her.''

''I'm sure you'll think of some way to deal with it, milady,'' the housekeeper said confidently. ''Is there anything in the way of supplies that you need us to send over to the priory?''

''Only the cakes and things for tea and sweets for after dinner. Now, do be sure to keep a list of all that we owe to the manor, for I wouldn't like to be in the earl's debt any longer than I can help.'' She looked down at her plate and realized that she had just eaten a poached egg and two slices of toast without even realizing it—putting herself even further into debt with Jethro, if he should have a mind to make a reckoning, which she doubted very much.

She rose. "I'll be getting back, then. Don't be afraid to send me a note if there's anything you simply cannot find, Mrs. Pennyfarthing, for I know I caused a lot of things to be moved around, and the maids will never remember where we put them all."

"You certainly did move things around, milady, but it's been years since the place smelled so fresh and clean. The earl doesn't know how much he is in your debt, never mind you being in his." The housekeeper had risen also, and now steered Sarah toward the front door, for as they passed him earlier she heard Rivers grumbling about ladies who didn't know their place and used the servants' entrance.

She had, of course, been seeking to avoid Jethro, and suddenly her efforts were in vain, for a door opened and her nemesis almost knocked her over as he stepped back into the hall.

"Pardon me, Cousin Sarah," Jethro murmured. "We really should stop bumping into each other quite like this or I'll be accused of trying to do you an injury."

"Good morning, Cousin Jethro. I had thought that you would be off with Robert by this hour or I would, of course, have come in to pay my respects," Sarah said in confusion, for he had truly taken her by surprise. She did not notice the housekeeper slip quietly away.

"You mean, of course, the way you always do when you come to the manor," he said, teasing her for deliberately avoiding him. "I'm very glad we met, however, for I was informed of something the other day that troubled me considerably. When I was complimenting Mrs. Pennyfarthing on the exceptionally fine condition of the house, she told me that shortly before I arrived you wore yourself to the nub getting this place cleaned from top to bottom."

Sarah looked extremely guilty. "It had not received a

thorough turning-out in many years, and I did not want you to realize how careless I had been in this regard," she said, not meeting his eyes.

He reached out a hand, placing one finger under her chin and forcing her to look directly at him.

"That's better," he said softly. "I am quite unused to seeing you embarrassed, and there is really no need, for I am the one who feels shame for putting you to so much trouble. I know only too well that the person who supervises an operation works twice as hard as anyone else. No wonder you bit off my head that first evening, for you must have been completely tired out."

His voice was soft and held a note of tenderness that, combined with the warmth of that finger beneath her chin, was playing havoc with her emotions. She was much afraid he could read her feelings in her eyes, for they had been known to betray her on other occasions, so she closed them and felt his finger trail from her chin to one hot cheek.

"Though I wish you hadn't gone to so much trouble, I do thank you, my dear, for I confess I've never known a house that gave off such a welcome."

"I'm glad you like it so well," she breathed, then added, "and I must go now, for I'm expected back at the priory very shortly."

She almost raced out of the house and into the woods, but soon set herself a slower pace for the walk back to the priory. With a deliberate effort, she put the last few minutes out of her mind for now, for she did not want to think about the feelings Jethro had aroused.

As she passed the stables, she recalled seeing Meg there earlier, and made herself give serious thought to the problem of her half-sister. She knew that Lady Pelham had little patience or undertanding of a teenage girl, for Sarah could still clearly recall how unhappy she herself had been when going through that most awkward stage. She had actually contemplated running away from home, and might even have done so had it not been for Rob.

He had teased her one day until she was in tears, a rare occurrence indeed, and then he had held her close and explained to her how the clumsiness and self-consciousness were just a part of growing up. He compared her to one of the chicks in a nest they had been watching ever since the eggs hatched. How awkward they had been when they first tried to fly, but how graceful once they had mastered it and took to the air, soaring and gliding above.

She determined to have a word with him, for she knew that Meg looked up to Robert and would listen more readily to him than she would to anyone else.

Her opportunity came that evening when the ladies were about to retire to the drawing room for their tea.

"Would you mind if I steal Sarah for an hour?" he asked Adele, purely as a matter of courtesy. "A few matters have arisen with the estates that she probably can answer more easily than anyone else."

Lady Pelham smiled and nodded, beckoning Meg and Bryan to come with her and Aunt Agatha.

George came in a moment later with a tray of tea; then, after placing the port decanter and glasses in front of Robert, he left, closing the door quietly behind him.

Sarah smiled and raised her eyebrows. "I cannot imagine what sort of matters can have come up that only I can answer," she said curiously, "but I am glad to have a chance to talk with you alone, for it must be days since we had the opportunity."

Robert grinned. "It's nothing serious. Just a question as to whether Percy gave instructions to have the field behind the home woods left fallow this year or not. As nothing was planted there last year, it would seem a little odd to just plow it and leave it again, but Jim Bennett swears that Percy told him to do so."

"And it would be one less field for him to worry about, other than seeing that it is plowed," Sarah added knowingly. "I'm quite sure that Percy always strictly rotated the crops, and though I did not hear him give specific instructions, I see no reason why you, or rather, Jethro, should not just tell Bennett that he has other plans.''

Robert grinned. ''That's what we hoped you would say, for we have received the distinct impression that the less Bennett has to work, the happier he is. No doubt Percy kept him on for personal reasons and knew to keep a watchful eye on him. I'll let Jethro know in the morning,'' he said. ''And now, tell me how you've been going along. You were looking a bit seedy the other day, I thought, but tonight, I must say, you're in the best of looks. Are you finally settling down here?''

She shook her head. ''I don't know if I ever really will, for as you know, I took this place in dislike the first time I saw it, and have not changed my mind one whit since. But you have no need to worry, for I don't mean to make a fuss about it,'' she assured him, then smiled softly. ''I walked over to see Mrs. Pennyfarthing this morning and she told me all is going well at the manor and that, so far, Jethro is the easiest of masters.''

''I'm not at all surprised, for I'm really enjoying helping him, and am glad that you called me in when you did. He's no one's fool, however, and could be very tough with anyone who crossed him, I believe,'' he added.

''Yes, I'm sure he could,'' Sarah agreed, then plunged into what she had been waiting to talk with him about. ''As I walked back this morning, I was thinking of how kind you were to me when I was a youngster, letting me trail around after you and teaching me how to do a lot of things girls did not, as a rule, have the opportunity to learn. And then when I reached that awkward age, you let me know that you understood exactly what was going on inside of me, and actually stopped me running away from home, though you probably did not realize it at the time.''

''I realized it,'' he said grimly, ''because two years before, I'd been ready to do the same thing myself. Adele meant well, I'm sure, but she had no idea how to bring up teenage youngsters.''

"She still doesn't, Rob, and I believe that Meg is having a difficult time right now. I'm not close enough to her anymore, but I was wondering if you might agree to talk with her and give her some of that wonderful advice you gave me." She saw that he was about to say something, and put in quickly, "I saw her early this morning hanging around the stables of the manor, and when she saw me coming, she disappeared into the woods. Mrs. Pennyfarthing tells me that she is there most mornings, trying to get a glimpse of Jethro. Apparently she has developed a girlish *tendre* for him strong enough to make her get up early each morning just to watch him ride off."

Her brother looked serious. "So that's what you were leading up to," he said a little grimly. "Something must be done, I suppose, for it doesn't look as though Adele is planning to leave with them anytime soon."

"I'm afraid not." She looked at him appealingly.

Suddenly he grinned. "All right. I'm not going to promise it will have any effect, but I will see what I can do to help her get over what is so often a bad time for a youngster. I'd best say that I saw her, though, for I'm quite sure she'd not take kindly to your having talked with me about her."

Sarah rose, and he got up and came over to her. "Playing the little mother, are you?" he asked, then added, "What a pity it is that you and Percy never had any children, for they would have been such a comfort to you at this time."

For just a moment Sarah thought of telling him, then decided he had enough on his mind without worrying about her also. He would know soon enough anyway.

They left the dining room arm in arm and walked slowly up the stairs together, for it was most likely that Lady Pelham had retired for the night by now. When they reached her bedchamber, he opened the door for her, dropped a kiss on her forehead, and bade her a good night.

"Have sweet dreams, and don't worry about that matter anymore, for I promise I'll do what I can about it," he added, then turned around and made his way back down the stairs and into the study.

Betty was waiting for her inside the bedchamber, and it was such a relief to let the maid undress her and brush her hair. While the bristles caressed her hair, she thought of her meeting this morning with Jethro, and realized that he had neither done nor said anything that should have caused her to feel so warm. It was probably the closeness of the hall and her own body, which was doing rather strange things lately, so she dismissed it as of no consequence and vowed to remain quite impersonal when next they met.

Betty helped her into bed, for she suddenly realized that she was very tired tonight, but once there, sleep did not come readily. She started to think of the child she was now sure she was carrying, and smiled softly, touching her stomach lightly, wondering what it looked like at this stage, and if it was a girl or a boy. Suddenly she did not feel quite as alone. Percy would have been so proud, she thought, and then, quite unexpectedly, tears started to stream down her face. She buried her head in the pillow and cried for the good, kind-hearted man who would now never know his child, and for the child who would never know its own father.

The tears stopped as quickly as they had started, and then she lay there thinking how unfair it was that, because it would be born after Percy's death, everything it should have owned had gone to a distant cousin instead. If it was a girl, it wouldn't matter, but if it was a boy it seemed so terribly unjust.

Mr. Musgrave would be coming soon to see Jethro about arranging an allowance for her, and she could talk with him about it, she supposed, but she had not been invited to meet with them and, in any case, did not feel that she wanted anyone to know her secret as yet. Not prone to superstition as a rule, she somehow felt that if she were to tell anyone except Betty about the baby, it might disappear and that terrible, lonely feeling would return.

There was really no need to tell anyone yet, for she could

still remember that when Adele had had Meg and, particularly, Bryan, neither she nor Rob had suspected until about three months before they were born. And these days, with the high-waisted gowns that everyone wore, it might be even longer before anyone guessed her condition. After all, she would soon be alone here except for Aunt Agatha, and, being in mourning, would not be entertaining or going out much for some considerable time.

6

Sarah was quite in error in believing that she would not be invited to take part in the meeting with the solicitor. When Jethro received word of the day and time the solicitor would be there, he sent a note to Sarah at once, asking if it was her wish to be present at the meeting or whether she might prefer that her brother represent her.

After lengthy consideration, she finally decided that Rob should go in her stead, for it would be most embarrassing to sit there while a decision was reached as to how much would constitute an equitable allowance. Perhaps, in her absence, Jethro might be more generous than if she were present, she thought.

In the event, however, she had no reason whatsoever to feel that he was being ungenerous toward her, for he agreed to furnish her with the present servants even though her household would soon be considerably smaller, to continue to pay for all the costs of food, and to furnish her with a carriage whenever she might have the need for one. As the priory was still a part of the estate, he would, of course, take care of its maintenance and repair.

In addition, she was to receive a personal allowance which she knew to be more than twice the amount needed for gowns and such. The money would be placed in an account for her use and, much to her surprise, she would be able to draw on it directly whenever she wished and not have to do so through Jethro. The latter arrangement, she understood from Rob, had been entirely Jethro's idea, for he knew that she had an excellent head for figures.

Regrettably, there was no possible hope of keeping the terms of the settlement from Lady Pelham without refusing outright to tell her, and as Sarah had no wish to hurt her stepmama in such a way, she briefly outlined the agreement to her.

"I feel quite sure," Lady Pelham said with the most satisfied of smiles on her face, "that the presence here of your family, giving you comfort in your time of need, has done much to persuade Jethro to be so generous. You showed unusual good sense in allowing Robert to represent you in the meeting with the solicitor, for there's no doubt, had you been there, you would have said something you should not. With your papa gone, it's a good thing Margaret has proved more biddable than you were, or I don't know what I would have done."

Sarah said nothing, for she had no intention of telling Adele that she should pay more attention to her own daughter. Instead she just hoped that Rob would be successful in persuading their sister to cease making an idiot of herself.

"I had half-decided we should leave at the end of the week," Lady Pelham went on, and Sarah knew to her sorrow what was coming next, "but now that things are settled, I believe we will stay another fortnight at least, for there has been such a marked improvement in Bryan's behavior since Jethro took him in hand. It must, of course, be the military training, for he pays little heed to Robert, as you know."

"It's more likely the fishing than anything else," Sarah said dryly. "When Bryan is over at the manor, he doesn't dare go racing around the place or interrupting Jethro in his study as he used to with me. I dropped by the stream late one afternoon and saw them there, but the only sounds to be heard were the birds twittering in the trees and an occasional fish jumping in the water. Jethro has somehow convinced Bryan that noise frightens the fish away, so he doesn't dare say a word.''

"The earl will make a wonderful father someday," Lady Pelham said, "for he has just the right touch. Does he have younger brothers and sisters?''

"I believe so," Sarah thought for a moment. "I think he said he had two brothers and a sister, but I don't recall how much younger they are."

Lady Pelham nodded sagely. "That accounts for it, then. He must have had a lot of practice dealing with young boys. I don't know how you got off on the wrong footing with him, my dear. It must have been your fault, for I've always found him to be completely agreeable and utterly charming each time we have met. The day will come, mark my words, when you'll be sorry you have not kept a tighter rein on that tongue of yours, and you'll find yourself completely in the suds.''

Sarah decided it was time to change the subject or she would most certainly be in the suds with her stepmama. "Aunt Agatha should be down for tea very shortly. Do you expect Meg to join us?'' she inquired.

"I really don't know," Lady Pelham said with a weary sigh. "Between the two houses, it's really most difficult to know where everyone is going to be at any time. Meg has started to take long walks about the property, and you might really think she would work up an appetite with it, but apparently it seldom has that effect upon her.''

Sarah need not have asked. She was quite sure that Meg would come in today, for she had invited Jethro to come over and have a look at the priory, and to take tea with them first. She regretted not asking him before, for he seemed extremely pleased when she had extended the invitation and, after all, it was a part of the estate he had inherited. He would be here in half an hour.

"If you'll excuse me, Adele, I'll go and speak to Cook about supper this evening," she said. "The last time she prepared duck it was a little too fatty for my taste, and I want to be sure it doesn't happen again.''

Lady Pelham nodded, then picked up the novel she had been reading, but a moment later the doorbell sounded and George came into the drawing room.

''Sir Malcolm Howard is here, milady,'' he said, adding, ''He was a good friend of the late earl's. Her ladyship did say she would be back in a moment, and . . .''

Lady Pelham gave a helpless shrug. ''And there's nowhere else in this place where he can wait, you mean. By all means, show him in here, George.''

The gentleman who entered a few minutes later appeared to be in his middle thirties, and was stylishly dressed in a blue kerseymere coat, light blue waistcoat, quite simply tied cravat, and buff pantaloons.

Lady Pelham held out her hand. ''Do come in, Sir Malcolm. I'm Lady Pelham and I have been visiting my stepdaughter and trying to be of as much help to her at this time as I can.''

He took the hand and bent low over it. ''I am delighted to meet you at last, my lady,'' he said in a smoothly cultured voice. ''I was proud to consider the late earl one of my closest friends, despite the difference in our ages, and I, also, mean to do everything I can to help your daughter through this painful time.''

Lady Pelham's eyebrows rose a fraction and she looked at him a little more closely.

''She will return in just a moment, I am sure, Sir Malcolm. I have usually an excellent memory for faces, but I do not recall having seen you here before,'' she murmured. ''I suppose I must have been out when you called.''

Before he had time to reply, however, Sarah hurried in. ''Malcom, how very nice of you to come by,'' she said, smiling warmly. ''Did you just get back from town? How is your dear mama?''

''I got back last evening, so you see that I wasted no time in coming to find out how you are going along, my dear.

I must say that you look much better than you did at the funeral, but of course that might be said of all of us who loved Percy. Such a tragic waste,'' he intoned.

Anxious to change the subject, she said, ''I see you have already met my stepmama, Lady Pelham, and I believe I hear my great-aunt, Lady Ramsbottom, in the hall.'' She made the introduction a moment later when Aunt Agatha entered the drawing room, and added, ''I'm happy to tell you that Lady Ramsbottom is going to live with me here at the priory to bear me company.''

He charmed the old lady by giving her his arm and escorting her to her favorite chair near the fire, then helping her to settle comfortably into it.

''I'm particularly glad you came by today, Malcolm,'' Sarah told him, ''for Lord Newsome, the new earl, will be joining us for tea, and I don't believe he has become acquainted with any of his neighbors as yet.''

''I trust he is continuing things the way Percy did, for I used to tell him that I never saw an estate so well-run. But the new earl is quite young, I understand, and probably not at all interested in following the old ways.'' He frowned. ''There'll be a lot of young officers like him coming back from the wars soon, for it is believed in political circles that the war may be over at any time—it's just a matter of deciding the terms of surrender. And then the country will likely be beset with young men who have been given authority beyond their years and no longer want to take orders from their betters.''

Robert and Jethro entered the drawing room just in time to hear the last of Sir Malcolm's remarks, and Jethro glanced sharply at the speaker but made no comment until the introductions had been performed.

He then said quietly, ''I could not help overhearing your last remarks, Sir Malcolm, and must beg to differ with your conclusion. Those young officers have been taking orders from the ones above them for a number of years, and should not cause any difficulties to speak of. The trouble will start when the enlisted soldiers return, for there'll be few jobs available for the strong and able, and none for the ones who have lost limbs serving their country.''

There was a new respect in Sir Malcolm's eyes as he nodded his head slowly. ''Of course, you are quite right, sir. I had not thought of it from that point of view. Tell me, how are you enjoying this part of England?''

Jethro murmured his thanks to Sarah as he took the cup of tea she handed to him; then he placed himself in a position where he could watch her graceful movements while replying to Sir Malcolm.

''Very much indeed. The land is rich and yields far more to the acre than is possible up north. The climate is kinder, also.'' He paused, watching how frequently the other man's glance went to Sarah. ''Am I correct in assuming you come from these parts, sir?''

Sir Malcolm nodded. ''Yes, but my property is nowhere near the size of yours, I'm happy to say. Our lands join in the middle of the woods to the south of here, and I have sufficient to keep me occupied, without having to devote all my time to its upkeep.''

While they talked, Meg had come into the room and Sarah set her to work passing plates of cakes and pastries around and bringing cups for refill. The girl stood now in front of Jethro, her blue eyes large and a deep flush on her cheeks, as she proffered a tray of small cakes.

He reached out and took one, thanked her, then said to Sir Malcolm, ''Have you met Margaret, sir, Sarah's sister?''

''Indeed I have not had that pleasure,'' the other man said, smiling kindly at the young girl. ''I had no idea that Sarah had such a lovely younger sister, for I was called to town just after Lord Mansfield's demise. Are you planning to stay and keep your sister company here?''

''No, I don't think so.'' Margaret's voice was so low that she could hardly be heard. ''I believe Aunt Agatha is going to remain after we leave, but I hope that won't be for a long time, for I just adore it here.''

Looking across at the trio, Sarah could not help but feel irritated with her stepmama for failing to notice her sister's behavior. She did not wish to embarrass Meg by calling to her, so she poured another cup of tea and took it over herself to Jethro, who, she realized, was quite unused to drinking from such dainty teacups.

"I believe Aunt Agatha would like some more tea, Meg," she said quietly. "Would you mind going over to get her cup for me?"

As Meg left, Sarah glanced at Jethro and was sure she saw a look of relief in his eyes before she turned and resumed her place at the tea urn.

It was not until Sir Malcolm was on the verge of leaving, and Sarah was about to give Jethro the promised tour of the priory, that young Bryan came hurrying in.

"I think you'd best eat your tea in the kitchen, if Cook does not mind," Sarah started to say, knowing that if the staff could not clear the tea things away now, it would mean they would be behind with dinner preparations.

Lady Pelham protested. "I'm sure he completely forgot the time, Sarah. When you marry again and have children of your own, you'll have to learn to be more lenient with them.''

Bryan looked gleeful until he glanced at up Jethro's face; then he said brightly, "It's all right, Mama. I'd much rather have tea in the kitchen," and hurried off in that direction before any more was said.

Lady Pelham sighed heavily, then turned to Meg. "Why don't you go with Sarah and Jethro, my dear," she suggested. "I'm sure you would rather do that than listen to two old ladies talking about fashions.''

Before her sister could answer, Sarah put in quickly, "I'm sorry, but I have some business matters to discuss with Jethro, Meg. I'm sure you can find something else to occupy you until dinner, for you're not usually even here at this hour.''

Ignoring her stepmama's frown, she turned to Jethro and said quickly, ''We'll start at the back of the house and work our way forward, I think,'' then led him into the hall.

Jethro's soft chuckle made her turn as they reached the door leading to the servants' wing.

''I didn't realize how good you were at tactical maneuvers,'' he told her, smiling broadly. ''I could have used you to get me out of a few tight spots in Spain.''

''She's very young and needs Adele to talk with her, but I'm afraid my stepmama appears to have blinders on as far as both of her children are concerned,'' she said with a sigh.

''It's not the first time, and it probably will not be the last.'' He grinned. ''But I'm willing to bet you were much more mature at her age.''

She shook her head. ''You'd lose your money, for I was even more awkward than Meg, in fact. But I do recall it was the only time in my life that I seriously contemplated running away from home—and not with a man, if that's what you were thinking. Had it not been for Rob, I would have surely done so.''

They walked along a passage to a door at the end, and Sarah fumbled in the pocket of her gown to produce a large key, which she handed to Jethro.

''This is the entrance to the cellars, which appear to be quite clean and dry, and excellent for storing food and such. A candle and flint are left on a ledge just inside the door, but for the moment there's nothing much to come down here for except the wines that you were kind enough to send over.

''I'd hate to be here alone, though there's nothing particularly eerie about the place. I always have the feeling, however, that there are secret passages leading out of the main cellar, and that we cannot find them because we don't know which secret place to press on the wall," she said with a wide grin.

"What an interesting idea," Jethro said with a chuckle. "I suppose you also feel that the passages lead up to some of the bedchambers, perhaps. If we were on the coast, you would imagine them going down to secret caves, and perhaps find a smuggler hiding in your bedchamber one night."

"What a quite dreadful idea, Cousin Jethro," Sarah declared, delighted that he had continued her own imaginings. "I promise you I'll examine the paneling in my own chamber very carefully tonight, just to make sure there is not a secret entrance to it."

Jethro had lit the candle and they walked quietly along until they came to where the wines had been stored, and noted that some cheeses and meat had also been added.

"It appears to be dry enough, which is what I was mainly worried about," Jethro said, "for I wouldn't like to think of you living somewhere where you could end up with rheumatism or worse."

Retracing their steps, they closed and locked the cellar door and went up the back stairs, used mostly by the servants. A door at the top led directly into a hall that ran the length of the house, with bedchambers off both sides.

"I would seriously doubt that the wood paneling was here when the monks were, but the arrangement of rooms appears to be consistent with, but probably little more than a part of, the original priory," Jethro remarked. "Don't you find the bedchambers very small?"

"Yes. Although at least half of the walls seem to have been removed at some time," she explained, "making each room twice as large. But even then, they're not very big, which is why it is a little cramped here with so many people in residence."

"I should think it would be," he exclaimed. "Why don't you have Robert and Bryan move over to the manor? It would make much more room for you here."

A feeling of gratitude at his generosity swept through her, but she knew better than to accept. "I'm very much afraid that if this place is made more comfortable, Adele will take up permanent residence," she said regretfully. "But I do appreciate the offer, Cousin Jethro."

She looked up into his eyes, and saw in them such genuine warmth that she felt the oddest sensation, as though something had jumped inside her. Did hearts really skip beats sometimes? she wondered. Then she told herself firmly that she was a recent widow, probably bearing her late husband's child, and she should be ashamed of herself for having such strange thoughts at this time.

"I suppose that I should at least speak to you of some business matter, having told Adele that I would be doing so. However, all I can think of at the moment is how generous you were with regard to an allowance for me. I meant to thank you for your kindness," she told him softly, placing a hand on his arm.

"It was little enough, when you've lost so very much because of Percy's early demise," he said, covering her hand with his. "Please don't think of it as being anything out of the ordinary, for it really is not, Cousin Sarah."

She smiled her thanks, then led him down the front staircase, where George was waiting with his hat and cane.

"You walked?" she asked in surprise.

"Do you think you're the only one who thinks it too short a distance to take the carriage?" he teased. "I'll have you know that I mean to walk a good deal when spring comes around, for I'll not allow myself to turn into a fat country gentleman."

She laughed. "You'll never be that—I mean fat, not a gentleman," she tried to explain, but it still sounded quite peculiar.

"I'd leave it alone if I were you," he told her, "for you seem to be as good at putting your foot in your mouth as I am."

He took her hand in his to thank her for tea and wish her a good afternoon, and after he left she looked at the hand as if she had not seen it before, then turned and ran back up the stairs to her chamber.

7

Sarah was now starting to feel very well indeed, and there was, in fact, an added sparkle in her eyes and a special glow in her cheeks. Even Lady Pelham remarked on it as they sat sipping coffee after luncheon one day.

"You must be a late bloomer, my dear," she said, a little more kindly than usual. "I don't recall ever seeing you in such good looks. It's not because of that gentleman who called the other day, is it?"

"If you mean Sir Malcolm Howard, of course it's not, Adele, for he has never been more than just a good friend of Percy's. He's been most kind to me since Percy died, but I'm sure there's nothing more to it than that," she told her. "At least, I hope that it's so on his part also, for I could never think of him as anything other than just a friend."

"He's a widower, isn't he?" Lady Pelham snorted. "That sort is always on the lookout for a likely young wife, particularly if he's childless."

Sarah appeared to consider it for a moment, then shook her head. "He is childless," she admitted, "but surely if he'd been looking for a wife he would have found one before now. In any case, he's simply a neighbor and a fine gentleman who has been kind and considerate, and as such, I will always make him welcome in my home."

"You could do worse, my dear, for he's a good-looking man, but I have to admit that I'd not like to see you sink from being the wife of an earl to that of a knight," her stepmama said, looking more than a little perturbed at the very idea.

"I have no wish to remarry unless I were to find someone I really loved," Sarah said softly, "and if that should be the case, I would not care were he just a plain mister."

Lady Pelham's scornful laugh rang out. "Where on earth did you get such a ridiculous notion, my girl? People like us never marry for such a foolish reason. I suppose you must have been reading too many of those silly novels that Mrs. Radcliffe writes. You must certainly marry again once you're out of mourning, and I shall consider it my duty to see that you find a completely suitable gentleman of rank."

She eyed Sarah thoughtfully. "As a dowager countess," she began, but stopped when Sarah started to laugh.

"Don't you think I am a little young to call myself a dowager, Adele?" she asked, smiling broadly.

"As the widow of a man of rank and property, that is most certainly what you are," Lady Pelham said firmly. "Though you may decide to still call yourself the Countess of Mansfield until Jethro takes a wife, and then perhaps change it to Sarah, Lady Wyndham, it does not alter the fact that you are the dowager."

"I know," Sarah said, still amused, "but it makes me feel quite ancient. And I notice that you don't call yourself the dowager Lady Pelham."

"I may very well do so when Robert marries," Lady Pelham retorted, "but as I was saying, as a dowager countess you can do much to help secure a good marriage for Margaret next year, if you will but bestir yourself, and we might even look for someone for you at the same time. I'm sure the earl would not mind your using the London town house if he does not need it himself. You never did have a come-out, and I know you cannot help but enjoy all the parties and gaiety of London in the Season."

There was a pause, but when Sarah made no comment, Lady Pelham went on, "Of course, I feel sure that since you now have such a very generous allowance, you will be only too glad to help with the cost of Margaret's gowns. After all, your dear papa paid all the expenses of your wedding, and as a result we were in quite straitened circumstances for some time afterward."

Sarah was simply horrified by the whole idea; then she suddenly remembered her present situation and wanted to laugh out loud, for by next year she would be too busy looking after a small son or daughter to fall in with Adele's plans.

"It's far too soon to make decisions of that sort," she murmured, trying her best to control the laughter that was threatening to bubble over inside of her. "We'll have to see how things stand when the time comes. Correct me if I'm wrong, Adele, but what you would like is for the earl to provide the London house and servants, and for me to pay for all the clothes, isn't it? Are you not overlooking the small matter of food and a town carriage?" she asked, carefully schooling her features to hide her amusement.

Lady Pelham was not easily deceived. "A Season in London might be pleasurable, and it might even be exhausting, but I can see nothing so obviously amusing about it. You always did have a very expressive face, my dear, and I would very much like to know what I said that caused you such hilarity."

Now in complete control, Sarah smiled disarmingly. "We have managed to rub along reasonably well over the years, Adele. Let's try to keep it that way and not probe too deeply into each other's feelings," she suggested. "When the time comes to bring Margaret out, I will, of course, do what I can to help her—short of marrying some old marquess . . . or was it a duke in his dotage that you had in mind for me?"

She rose gracefully, quite sure that her condition did not show in the slightest under her fashionably high-waisted gown, though she was sure that she could now see a slight but quite distinct rounding of her stomach when she disrobed.

"Did Robert say how long he expected to be away?" she asked, turning as she reached the door.

"If he had told anyone, it would have been you, surely," Lady Pelham snapped, "for the two of you have always been as thick as thieves."

Sarah gave a slight shrug, considering the remark not worthy of comment, then stepped back as George's knock sounded on the door.

He came inside and closed the door behind him. "Mrs. Lofthouse is asking for just a moment of your time, milady," he said quietly. "Shall I show her into the study?"

"You can see her in here, Sarah," Lady Pelham said sharply, "for I'm just leaving, but I would recommend you give her short shrift, for she is decidedly not the kind of person you should be associating with."

Sarah raised her eyebrows at her stepmama's uncivil remark in front of a servant, but that lady brushed quickly past her and out of the room.

"By all means ask her to come in, George," Sarah said quietly, "and I'll ring if we need anything."

Mrs. Lofthouse entered a few minutes later. She was gowned today in a deep shade of puce, with matching plumes on her large hat.

"I'll not keep you, my dear," she said, still trying to catch her breath after hurrying from her carriage, "for with your family here I know you must have a thousand and one things to do. But I felt I must warn you that Florence Kendal has just returned to the area, and she's been asking a lot of questions about the new earl."

Sarah could not help but smile. "I believe he is more than capable of taking care of himself, Lillian," she said, "but wasn't she chasing after Sir Malcolm this time last year? I'm sure I recall Percy teasing him about it."

"That she was, to be sure, but Sir Malcolm knows how to handle one of her sort," the stout lady attested, still breathing heavily.

"And you don't think Lord Newsome does?" Sarah asked. "I feel sure he must have met many women of Florence's sort in the army. And in any case, it's really none of my concern whom he chooses to associate himself with." She tried to sound more disinterested than she felt.

"Well, you can be sure she'll be over here in no time at all, trying to find out everything she can about him from you. You see, no one can tell her anything, for he's completely unknown hereabouts. You're right, though, now I think on it, for he can't have risen to the rank of colonel without knowing how to go along." She put up a hand and touched Sarah's face. "It's nice to see a bit of color back in your cheeks. Is there any truth in the rumor I've been hearing?"

A puzzled frown creased Sarah's brow. "What rumor is that, Lillian? I suppose I'm the very last to hear such things these days."

"That you might be carrying the late earl's child," Mrs. Lofthouse said bluntly. "I think the story came from your little brother."

Now Sarah was indeed surprised. She had been about to blame her maid, Betty, for having revealed her secret, but if it came from Bryan, then her stepmama just had to be behind it.

"Do you think you might try to quash it for the time being?" she asked earnestly.

The plumes waved gaily as Mrs. Lofthouse shook her head quite decidedly. "There's no stopping that kind of talk, my dear. If it's true, you might just as well admit it, for that's the only thing that'll put an end to the gossiping. Is it true?" she asked bluntly.

Sarah nodded.

"Well, it looks as if we're going to have a very interesting summer this year," Mrs. Lofthouse said with a chuckle. "If there's anything I can do to help, just let me know."

She prepared to rise, shaking her head as Sarah was about to come to her aid; then, positioning herself carefully, she heaved herself out of the chair and onto her feet. "Don't come to the door, my love, for I can manage very well on my own. And if the new earl doesn't already know your condition, you'd best tell him before someone else makes it sound like something it isn't.''

She made her way slowly to the door. ''Tell your stepmama how sorry I am that I missed her,'' she said with a deep chuckle; then she was gone, leaving Sarah extremely vexed, for she had not wanted anyone to know her secret just yet.

Jethro Newsome rode into the stables and dismounted. It had been a long day, for though there was still an hour or two of daylight left, he had set out before the sun rose. He had even regretted, earlier, not allowing young Bryan to come with him, for with Robert returned to his own estates for a few days, he missed his companionship.

What he would have liked even more was the company of the countess, but though they no longer came to cuffs every time they met, Sarah did not deliberately seek his company as, to his increasing displeasure, did young Margaret.

He was, at times, surprised at Lady Pelham's thoughtlessness where the girl was concerned, and on other occasions he wondered if she was being deliberately obtuse. But he was no Johnny Raw, and he did not intend to be caught in any parson's mousetrap. He made it a point not to seek conversation with Margaret except when others were close by to see and hear everything that was said.

''The fish are jumping all over the stream, Jethro.''

With a pleased smile, the earl turned to greet young Bryan, knowing he had probably been sitting there on the bench waiting for him for the last hour.

''Do you think they'll jump right onto our hooks?'' he asked, feigning exhaustion, ''for I'm not sure that I have the strength to even cast out the line.''

''You could just come and watch me, if you like,'' Bryan said eagerly, ''and I'll give you half of my catch.''

Jethro reached out a hand and ruffled the young boy's hair.

"Give me ten minutes, and I'll be right with you," he said. "My rod is in the back of the stables, if you'd like to get it for me."

In his chamber he quickly threw water on his face to refresh himself, then returned to where the boy patiently waited. The two of them strolled companionably down to their favorite part of the stream, where they could cast without getting the lures tangled in overhanging trees, and settled themselves comfortably upon the bank.

If the fish were not exactly jumping all over the stream, there was an occasional splash, and they had each caught a good-size trout before Bryan broke the silence.

"Jethro, do you ever hear people say things that you don't understand?" the youngster asked.

"All the time," the earl said with a grin, "and when they do, I usually ask them to speak plain English."

Bryan looked decidedly guilty. "But if they don't know you heard them, you can't very well ask them that, can you?"

"You're right there, boy. It would be impossible to do so without revealing yourself. Did you ever think they might sometimes know you're listening, and deliberately say things to confuse you?"

The youngster grinned sheepishly and looked down at his rod. "Yes, Sarah and Rob do it all the time, but Rob's away, and it was Sarah that was being talked about."

The earl's ears immediately pricked up and he hesitated only a moment before saying, "If it was something unpleasant, I don't think I want to hear it."

Bryan's eyes opened wide and he shook his head vehemently. "It wasn't anything nasty. I wouldn't repeat nasty things about Sarah to anybody," he said, quite indignant at the idea.

"All right then. What was it?" Jethro asked, now more than a little curious himself.

"Mama said that she thought Sarah was in an interesting condition," he blurted out, "and that doesn't make any sense to me."

Jethro looked grim. Then he wondered if perhaps the youngster had not heard properly.

"Are you sure that's what she said? Nothing else?" he asked.

"I heard it clearly, for the door was half-open and she was talking to Aunt Agatha, who is a little hard of hearing. She had to repeat it twice," Bryan asserted.

"Watch your rod," Jethro suddenly called, trying to distract the boy until he could think what to tell him. "I think you've got a nibble."

It was a lucky call, for a second later there really was a fish on the line, and it took all of Bryan's newfound knowledge to bring the quite large trout in. By then, as Jethro had hoped, Sarah's interesting condition was forgotten as Bryan expounded on the way he had caught the biggest trout ever. He was most unlikely to remember his sister's problem until some considerable time later.

The youngster ran eagerly back to the priory while Jethro made his way toward the manor, walking slowly as he wondered what difference, if any, Bryan's information might make to his inheritance.

There was, of course, always the possibility that Lady Pelham was mistaken, for it was obvious that Sarah had said nothing to anyone, but he clearly recalled how unwell she had seemed just after his arrival. As he had three young siblings, he was not completely unaware of the symptoms, if they might be classed as such, of the early stages of pregnancy.

For the first time since his return from Spain, he slept badly that night, and it was quite a relief when, halfway through breakfast, Robert appeared.

Jethro jumped up at once and pulled a chair out for him. "You can have no idea how glad I am to see you," he said with feeling. "When did you get back?"

Robert was obviously amused. "Just in time for dinner last night, and strange as it may seem, I received every bit as warm a welcome at the priory as I am getting from you now. I can see I'll have to go away more often."

"How did you find Sarah?" Jethro asked.

"It's funny you should ask," Robert said, "for I thought her in exceptional looks despite her black gowns. She seemed sort of pale and sickly just after Percy died, and I suppose that was only natural, but now she's positively blooming. Haven't you seen her lately?"

"Oh, yes, I've seen her and I agree with you completely," Jethro told him. "Has she said anything about being enceinte?"

Robert almost jumped out of the chair. "Did I hear you correctly?" he asked, quite obviously amazed.

The earl nodded. "Yes, you heard me, all right. My information came from young Bryan, who did not, and still does not, know what being in an interesting condition means."

"That young monkey is going to listen outside doors once too often and hear something he'd rather not have heard, one of these days," Robert pronounced. "Was it Adele who said it?"

"Yes, and she said it three times because she was talking to Lady Ramsbottom, so there's little chance that he misheard her." Jethro looked grim.

"I agree, although Aunt Agatha is not at all deaf, she just pretends to be when she does not want to hear what our stepmama has to say. Adele could, however, be mistaken," Robert said, "and it would certainly not be the first time, for she has always been inclined to jump to conclusions on insufficient evidence. I'll ask Sarah tonight if there's any truth in it."

Jethro shook his head. "Although I'd very much like to know, I'd rather you didn't, for I hate young Bryan to think me a talebearer," he said.

"All right, I won't, then, if you're trying to protect your source of information. It's more than likely that Adele will ask me when she gets me on my own, and then I can pass it on to Sarah without mentioning either you or Bryan.'' Just then Rivers came in with fresh coffee and rolls, and Robert thanked him and waited until he had left before continuing.

"Can I assume that if the legal question is not clear-cut, you would not try to fight my sister?'' Robert asked. "For I could hardly continue to help you here if that was your intention.''

"I think you'll find there's always a precedent,'' Jethro assured him, "and I've no wish to hurt Sarah, but neither will I back down if I am the rightful heir. However, as you know, I also inherited my father's estate, which my brother is presently taking care of, so I'm not exactly land poor. I must say, though, that if it is true, I cannot help but feel very annoyed with your sister for not informing me as soon as she was aware of a problem, and I will most certainly let her know about it.''

Robert did not appear at all concerned for his sister, but said, "If Adele is suspicious, I have a feeling things might come to a head rather quickly. Perhaps as soon as this evening. Why don't you join us for dinner tonight? One more will not make any difference, and it will be soon enough for me to let Sarah know you're coming when I get back to the priory this afternoon.''

Jethro readily accepted, for he was finding it exceedingly dull to dine alone every evening at the manor.

But when, later that day, Robert informed Sarah that there would be a guest for supper, she immediately became concerned and hastened to the kitchens to considerably augment the comparatively simple meal she had planned.

8

As the dowager Lady Wyndham, Sarah was much changed from the Honorable Sarah Pelham who, at twenty, had married the fifth Earl of Mansfield. Lord Percy had been an old friend of her papa's. She would at no time have been described as awkward or gauche, but without the advantage of a Season in London, she had lacked the polish, the self-assurance such an experience was meant to impart.

Her husband had been a kind, understanding man, and if they had not been in love when they married, they had at least grown to love each other in their own way, and he had taught her much. They were close, if a little like father and daughter, and it had seemed natural for him to show her the day-to-day running of the estate, which had proved so very useful after his sudden death. But he had also shown her the clothes that best suited her particular style, and explained why, which in turn had given her an added confidence.

Most important, however, he had insisted that she tackle any problem that came up fair and square before someone else could take it and, willfully or not, misconstrue it. He had liked the Lofthouses, and had not permitted anyone to denigrate them. Now she had cause to be grateful to Lillian, for by letting her know what was going on, she had given Sarah the upper hand.

She was not going to wait for Adele to start dropping hints to her. She meant to take the reins firmly in her hands and announce her condition this evening. It would no doubt cause problems with Jethro, for she did not expect him to know any more than she did as to what would happen to the earldom, but if rumors had already started, she had waited long enough.

"Which gown will it be this evening, milady?" Betty asked, then said slyly, "You've not worn the lace one yet, and I know you'll look well in it."

"Then most certainly get it out, for I mean to make an announcement this evening," Sarah said with a rather grim smile.

"I'm so glad, milady," the maid said, nodding. "I've been meaning to tell you that the servants are starting to hint about you, though I don't know where they can have heard, for it certainly was not through me."

"Someone has probably been watching you more carefully than you realized, and noticed the dry biscuits you now bring with my morning tray," Sarah said with a shrug. "But, no matter. I'll bring it out into the open tonight and stop all the talking behind my back."

A half-hour later, she left her chamber looking nothing short of regal. Her brown hair had been arranged in something closely resembling a coronet atop her head, and the scalloped edges of the black floral lace gown framed her neck to form a high V in the front, and then tantalizingly covered her completely, from shoulders to wrists and from the high neckline to her toes.

She had made a point of being several minutes late, for she wanted everyone to be there when she made her entrance into the drawing room. A swift glance around told her all were present except for Bryan and Meg, so she turned to the waiting George and said quietly, "You may close the door now for a few minutes," and stepped inside.

"Good evening, Jethro," she said, offering him her hand.

"I'm delighted that Robert thought to invite you this particular evening."

He looked surprised, but took her hand and raised it to his lips, then stood watching her, a slight smile twitching at the corners of his mouth. He knew her well enough by now to be sure that something was afoot.

Lady Pelham was seated in an armchair close to the fire, sipping sherry, and Aunt Agatha had taken the straighter chair she preferred, next to a card table. Robert was standing on the other side of the fireplace, watching her, and his eyebrows rose as though he, too, recognized that something unprecedented was about to take place.

"I'm glad you're all together, for I have a small announcement to make," Sarah said, speaking quietly but noticing that even Aunt Agatha seemed as though she could hear her quite clearly. "I have been waiting until I was absolutely sure before saying anything, but now I would like you all to know that I am enceinte—I am expecting the late earl's child. My only regret is that he never knew, for it would have made him the happiest of men."

Lady Pelham looked quite shocked. "But, my dear Sarah, this is hardly the thing to talk about in mixed company. If you had spoken to me first, I would have—" she started to say, but stopped when her stepdaughter raised a hand.

"On the contrary, Adele, as it concerns us all, particularly Jethro, I believe that I should be the one to tell him rather than wait until someone else hears a rumor and does so."

She saw Robert's cheeks flush a deep shade of pink, and was immediately sorry, for she had not wanted to embarrass him. She wondered who could have told him, and why he had not approached her about it.

Jethro did not look at all surprised, and the smile that had been on his face when she entered the room was still in place. From the way Robert glanced in his direction, she assumed that one of them had told the other a short time ago. Was this why Robert had asked Jethro to dinner?

Lady Ramsbottom rose and came over to her niece, placing her arms around her shoulders. "My dear, I am so happy for you. This is wonderful news, and I am only sorry that Lord Percy never knew. You must take great care of yourself, for you have someone else to think about now."

Not to be outdone, Lady Pelham declared, "That settles one problem for me. I was going to leave for home at the end of the week, but now I cannot possibly do so until after the child is born. At a time like this, a girl needs her mother, and I have certainly been all of that and more to you, Sarah."

"That is not necessary at all, Adele," Sarah said quickly, horrified at the thought of having the whole family with her for another five or six months. "I feel perfectly fine, and I shall have Aunt Agatha with me in case I need anything, and Jethro is, of course, only a short distance away."

"Don't argue with me, my dear, for you know it's no use when my mind is made up. Why, what would your dear papa have thought if I left you to have your first child alone? I'll send the carriage home tomorrow to bring back some more clothes and things, and some of those old recipes that did me so very much good when I had backaches and sickness."

"Adele, now I must remind you that there are gentlemen present," Sarah hissed. "I don't need anything or anyone at the moment. Why don't you go back at this time, and I'll send for you before the child is due?"

The older woman looked surprised that Sarah did not eagerly accept her decision; then she shook her head firmly. "You know nothing about a lying-in or anything else. I'm not leaving you, no matter what you say."

Over her stepmama's shoulder Sarah glimpsed the expression on Robert's face. He was quite obviously trying desperately not to laugh, and when he saw her looking at him, he wagged a wicked finger at her.

Jethro pointed to his glass of sherry and raised his eyebrows, and at Sarah's nod he picked up one from the tray and brought it over to her.

"Have you any idea what the law is in such a case?" he asked her quietly.

She took a sip of her sherry and slowly swallowed it before answering. "I really have not the remotest idea. I suppose much depends upon whether it is a boy or a girl. I would imagine that you'll want to speak with your solicitor and find out?" she suggested.

He nodded. "It would seem to put me in a rather awkward position, no matter what," he said, "and I have to admit that I'm none too pleased that you did not tell me before."

Sarah was angry, and it showed. "I thought I was being most considerate to tell you at this time," she snapped. "You heard Adele. She didn't think I should even discuss the matter in front of you."

"She's a fool and you are far from being one," he said quietly. "And now she means to take advantage of this in order to stay here and eat my food and use my servants."

"Did I not understand that all the servants presently at the priory were to stay on working for me after my family left?" she asked stiffly. "It would seem that you are already regretting your agreement."

"You couldn't be further from the truth. I made an agreement and I don't regret it, but I simply cannot abide that woman, and heartily dislike providing for her any longer than I must," he growled. "She's completely self-centered and is using you as a means to find a rich husband for Margaret, but you just can't see it."

Although Sarah was only too aware of this, she had no intention of agreeing with him, and he was, without exception, the most selfish, disobliging creature she had ever met, and she did not mean to let him speak so of her and her family.

"If she's looking after her own interests, Jethro, so are you also, or you'd not be upset that I did not tell you earlier about the baby. She's already told me that she wants me to sponsor Margaret in London once we're out of mourning, but you underestimate her ambitions. She also wants to marry me off again—or at least she did before she knew that I'm increasing.''

"With a young baby, you'll not be running around London next Season. But then, I wonder what any of us will be doing, for I've a strong feeling that a son would inherit,'' he said coldly. "That is, of course, if it really is Percy's child.''

It was fortunate that they were standing a little apart from the others and speaking quietly. Robert just happened to move in front of Lady Pelham at the crucial moment, so that she failed to see her stepdaughter's hand go back to slap the earl across the face, and how that gentleman thwarted the attempt by taking her wrist in a painful grasp.

"I believe that dinner must be ready, Sarah, for George has been trying to get your attention these last ten minutes or more,'' Robert said quietly, looking grimly at the pair of them as Jethro released his hold on her wrist. "Why don't you finish your discussion in the study afterward?'' he suggested. "And I will make a point of being there also, for it would seem you need someone to act as referee.''

Sarah wanted to rub her wrist, for his grip had been hard and it still hurt, but she would not give him the satisfaction of seeing her do so.

"I'm afraid it was my fault entirely,'' Jethro said smoothly. "I said something quite uncalled-for and I offer my sincere apology, my lady.''

He also offered his arm to take her in to dinner, and reluctantly she placed her hand lightly upon it, but they observed a stony silence for the short distance to the dining room and while he seated her at table.

The dinner, which she had augmented so happily once Rob had told her the earl was coming, tasted like ashes in Sarah's mouth. How dare he make such a suggestion! Was that what he was planning to talk to his solicitor about? Did he mean to make such insinuations in an effort to discredit her and keep the estates?

Suddenly she was glad that she had seated him at table next

to Adele. If he disliked her stepmama so much, he would be having as miserable a time as she was, and he deserved it.

It seemed an eternity before the meal ended and she could give the signal for the ladies and the younger ones to leave. But once they were in the drawing room, she knew that Adele would be full of questions she had no wish to answer.

"You know, my dear, I am so disappointed that I was not the first one you confided in," Lady Pelham said pettishly. "A little bird had told me that it might be so, and I would have so much preferred that it had come directly from you."

Sarah sighed. "I cannot imagine why, Adele, for it's really much too early to be discussing the matter, except for the problem of the inheritance. I made the announcement tonight because I felt it only fair to give Jethro a chance to go carefully into the matter."

"And you must also do so, I should think," Lady Pelham declared, "for you're surely not going to take whatever he tells you as being true? He is not exactly a disinterested party and might seek to retain the earldom against all odds."

"While we're on the subject, I just want to tell you again that I really would rather you go home at this time and take care of your duties there, Adele. I'm perfectly well—in fact, better in looks, I believe, than I have ever been, as you said yourself. You could return just before the baby is due."

Lady Pelham looked quite hurt. "You've always been like my own daughter to me, Sarah, and I'm surprised that you do not gracefully accept my offer to do what every mother would do at the prospect of the birth of her first grandchild. I am quite sure that if Percy had been alive he would have welcomed me staying on, and if I were to go home and something happened to cause you to lose the baby, I would never forgive myself." She produced a kerchief and dabbed at her eyes, though Sarah had yet to glimpse the first tear.

Young Bryan came over then to ask if he might stay up a little longer because the earl would be joining them shortly, and Lady Pelham said that of course he could, and told Margaret she might stay too, for she would soon have to get used to conversation with gentlemen and it would be good practice.

Suddenly Sarah felt exhausted, and with no desire to do the polite by Jethro any more this evening, she begged them all to excuse her.

"Of course, my dear," Lady Pelham said, eager to play the hostess in her stepdaughter's absence. "You've got to think of the little one now and get your rest, you know."

As she walked slowly up the stairs, Sarah distinctly recalled how Adele had behaved when she had been carrying Margaret. She had apparently considered herself quite fragile and had spent her days lying down either in her bedchamber or on a couch in the drawing room. Sarah had been quite young at the time, but she had been unable to help wondering how she could have been so very well one moment, and unable to perform even the smallest task the very next.

When the ladies left the dining room, Robert and Jethro settled back to enjoy a cigar and a glass of fine brandy in peace.

Once the ritual of preparing the cigars for smoking and the sampling of the mellow aged spirits was accomplished, Robert carefully cleared his throat and asked quietly, "Would you mind telling me why my sister became angry enough to try to slap you, in a room filled with people? It seems most unlike her."

Jethro took an enameled snuffbox out of his pocket and critically studied the painting on the lid. Then he flicked it open and offered it to Robert, who declined. After inhaling an infinitesimal pinch, he dusted his fingers, then looked at Robert.

"I said something I shouldn't have, and I don't intend to go into details, for she and I must deal with this ourselves. I think we'll do it best alone, though I've no doubt that she'd like to cut me up into little pieces right now, and feed me to the crows." Jethro pursed his lips as he considered how best to put it to this young man who had become such a good friend in just a few weeks.

"You see, Robert, it's a big problem for both of us, and can only be settled legally, no matter what we might personally like to do. I'm no expert on the law, so I believe I might go into London in the morning and have a talk with my own solicitor," he went on. "Not that I think he'll give me an answer, for I know how those fellows are. They ponder and look for precedents and try to run up as big a bill as they can." He sighed wearily, shaking his head.

"I know you apologized, Jethro, but I was so very proud of her when she came in, looking the handsomest I've seen her in an age, and calmly stopped all the guessing and talk. After that, the light seemed to go out in her again, and I'm afraid I blame you for it," Robert said frankly.

Jethro's grin was a little lopsided as he murmured, "She could have stopped conversation in any salon in London in that gown, yet there was nothing seductive about it. She really did look magnificent, but you've got to see my side of this mess also. I've spent two months already tending to these lands, with your most generous help. It might very easily work out that I spend another six months of my life putting them in the finest condition I can—then Sarah has a son who immediately inherits everything, lock, stock, and barrel."

Robert nodded. "I can see what you mean. And if you left right now and looked to your own lands for six months, this place would go to rack and ruin, for I can't stay much more than another week."

Jethro nodded in agreement. "And then, if a girl was born, or if the solicitors decided an unborn son could not inherit, I would come back and have to spend night and day for a year or more to set everything to rights again." Jethro rose and put a hand on the younger man's shoulders. "I know you must go, and one day I hope to pay back in kind for all you've done on my behalf."

He sighed. "I think it would be best if I don't join the ladies this evening, Robert, for I have no wish to upset Sarah any more than I have already. When we've finished here, I believe I'll leave. The walk back will be a good time to ponder the problem. I should return within three or four days at the most, and I promise to let you know at once whatever I find out.''

Ten minutes later they parted company in the hall. Because it was late, Robert wanted to send for the carriage, but Jethro would have none of it.

''The walk will be good for me, as I said. I do my best thinking that way. Please give my thanks to Sarah for a delicious dinner, and my apologies once more for causing her additional grief. It was the very last thing I wished to do to her this evening.''

By the time Jethro reached the manor, he knew that his decision was the right one. He had made an unforgivable implication to Sarah, and he would not at all blame her if she did not speak to him for a month, so the less she saw of him for now, the happier she was bound to be.

Never one to procrastinate, he gave immediate instructions to his former batman, now his valet, to be prepared to set out on horseback at dawn, then retired at once to get as much sleep as he could, for he meant to be in London before nightfall tomorrow.

9

When Sarah heard quite early the next morning that the earl had left for London at dawn, she hastened to the manor. She knew that its library contained a great many thick tomes on English law, and she meant to spend as much time as she had at her disposal to find out just what her child's position might be.

Arranging a half-dozen volumes on the large desk at which she had so often worked on the estate accounts, she opened up the first one to the subject of hereditary law. But it seemed to her that there was a vast number of different kinds of inheritances, and she had scarcely reached the middle of the first section before Mrs. Pennyfarthing came in with a luncheon tray filled with most of her favorite dishes.

"I just wanted to say, milady, that the staff here is delighted about your good news, and we all know how joyful the late earl would have been," she told Sarah, her round motherly face a picture of happiness. "If there is aught any of us can do to help, you only have to let us know."

Sarah smiled warmly. "That's very kind of you, but it's a long way off as yet, and my stepmama has indicated her intention of staying on," she said. "Please thank everyone, and you may be sure that if I need anything at all, I'll not hesitate to ask."

She nibbled on the savory pastries and slices of cold pheasant, and glanced for the first time around the room. At first she had thought that nothing had been changed, but then she realized that there were a few ornaments and things that had not been there before.

She walked over to a table by the window to examine more closely a miniature of a very pretty woman she at first thought must be a particular friend of the earl's, then realized from the portion of gown she could see that it was quite different from the ones worn today and that it was more likely to be Jethro's mother.

A dress sword in an ornate scabbard hung on one of the few empty places on the wall, and a leather-bound writing case lay on another table, but Sarah would not for a moment have thought of looking inside it.

She realized now that there was quite a number of personal items throughout the house, both hers and Percy's, that she should have removed when she left the manor, but she would not think of touching them now until the earl returned and she could let him see just what she was taking.

With a heavy sigh she went back to searching the books on law, and was unaware that a couple of hours had gone by until there was a knock on the door and she looked up to see Bryan's freckled face and big blue eyes peeking around the edge.

"Rivers said I wasn't to disturb you, Sarah, but Mama told me to find you and bring you back. She says a Lady Kendal has come to call," he said solemnly, adding, "an' do you think, after she goes, that you'd like to go fishing with me? I'll show you what to do."

Sarah had to smile as she stood up and stretched her cramped limbs. "I might just do that, young man, for I've been shut indoors all day, but first I have to see what Lady Kendal has called about."

They went out into the hall arm in arm, and Sarah wished Rivers a good afternoon and asked her to let Mrs. Penny-farthing know she would be back early tomorrow, and to please not move the books she had set out on the library table.

Bryan chattered all the way back to the priory, telling her once again about his performance in bringing in, last week, "the biggest fish in the stream." He made Sarah promise to meet him in an hour and a half, then hurried off before his mama saw him and insisted he come in to tea also.

Sarah entered the house through the back door and went up to her bedchamber to tidy up before coming downstairs to see the lady with whom Percy had once been extremely friendly before he decided to remarry. She could not blame Adele for sending for her at once, for though she herself now knew Florence Kendal quite well, she was also fully aware that she was not well-received by the local ladies.

The deep black which the faded blond lady wore was so intense that even Sarah, who was accustomed to her dramatics, almost asked if she had lost a loved one. Then Florence rose and flung her arms around her, almost smothering her in her zeal.

"Oh, Sarah, I was visiting my dear Charles's family when I heard the sad news, and wanted to come right away to commiserate with you, for I knew Percy so very well. Better than he knew himself at times," she avowed.

With quiet tolerance Sarah disentangled herself from the other woman's arms, seated her in a chair with her back to the bright window, and reached for the tea that young Meg had poured.

"You remembered that my weak eyes cannot stand the bright sunshine. How very thoughtful of you, my dear, at such a time," Lady Kendal murmured, sipping the tea slowly as her glance missed not one part of Sarah's appearance. "And now I understand you have given us all a little surprise."

Sarah's eyes sparkled with mirth and she could not resist replying, "Not yet, but I hope to do so in about six months' time."

"I must say that it seems to agree with you, for you look positively radiant. You must be feeling very happy indeed about it, but I suppose you have not yet completely considered all the implications." Lady Kendal gave her a thoughtful glance. "Have you?"

"Probably not, but I've no doubt you can enlighten me." Sarah's voice was soft, and Lady Pelham, listening intently, had to lean forward to catch every word.

"Well, of course, I never considered such a thing myself." Lady Kendal paused and smiled at Margaret as she took a piece of cake from the tray the girl had presented; then she busied herself cutting a small portion with her fork before continuing apologetically, "But it was when I was in the lending library the other day that I heard someone say how it would be best if the child were born a little early, for if it were late there would most certainly be talk."

"First babies quite frequently come late," Lady Pelham said quite decidedly.

"Of course they do, my lady," Lady Kendal said with a smile, "but you must agree that if the child did come early it would save a lot of unnecessary tongue-wagging. Is the earl in residence? I had hoped I might get the chance to meet him, but I suppose he is very busy."

"I understand he is not at home right now," Lady Pelham said firmly. "And when he is here he is usually very busy going over affairs of the estate with my stepson."

This time Lady Kendal's smile looked genuine, and a light came into her eyes. "Oh, yes, I did hear that Sarah's elder brother was here. What a pity I missed him also."

"He has little time to spend drinking tea with us ladies, for he is most anxious to get back to his own lands and to his affianced." A protective note had entered Lady Pelham's voice, but it was quite in vain, for just then Robert appeared in the doorway.

"Am I too late for tea?" he asked cheerfully, then paused. "I'm sorry, I didn't realize you had a visitor, Sarah, or I'd have taken the time to change from my dirt into something more respectable."

"Well, you're in now, so you may as well stay," Lady

Pelham said ungraciously before Sarah could say a word. "This is Lady Kendal, one of Sarah's friends . . . my stepson, Lord Pelham."

Sarah was actually quite relieved, for from the expression on her stepmama's face she half-expected her to say that Lady Kendal was just leaving, for she had already stayed the usual length of time. But she knew from experience that Florence would never leave while there was a man in the room, and it was always amusing to see her go into action the minute one came anywhere near.

She knew it to be common knowledge that Florence had once been a very good friend of Percy's before they had married, and she had no doubt that the woman was sorry about his death, but Florence was drawn to men as to a magnet, and simply could not help herself. Unhappily, few men were attracted by her for very long, but she always tried, and had recently taken to the discreet application of a little powder and paint to make her thirty years appear closer to twenty-five.

She was talking to Robert now, her eyes big again with unshed tears, and though Sarah could not catch all of the conversation, she assumed that she was expressing once more her deep sorrow at Percy's demise, and telling him of the deep regard in which she held Lord Wyndham.

Lady Pelham was frowning and trying to catch as much as she could of the conversation with her stepson.

Aunt Agatha, who had been watching the whole tableau with considerable interest, looked at Sarah, who could not resist slowly closing one eye in a broad wink. The old lady started to cough, making Sarah feel guilty for being the cause, so she went over to her and patted her back.

When the coughing spell was over, Sarah noticed the clock on the mantelpiece. It was almost time she left to meet Bryan, and she had no intention of disappointing the youngster.

"I do hope you will excuse me," she said, "but I promised to do something for Lord Newsome and I don't wish to be late."

Before any questions could be asked, she swiftly left the room and hurried up to her bedchamber to change her gown for something more suited to sitting on the bank of a stream. Then she left through the back door in case Adele should try to waylay her in the hall.

Bryan was waiting there, looking a trifle woebegone, as if he had feared she might not come, but when he saw her approaching, her grinned and waved wildly.

"I know what you were thinking," Sarah told him. "You thought I wasn't coming, and I must tell you that I left a room full of people to come and meet you here."

Bryan shrugged. "What's a room full of people compared to a chance to fish?" he asked. "You want me to show you how Jethro taught me?"

She nodded, knowing that she had just left herself open to an hour or more of "Jethro says." But if she did not have to see the man in person she could put up with that, she thought, deciding not to tell the boy that Percy had taught her to fish just after they were married, and that she had caught a lot of trout in this stream.

"Now, the first thing you have to do is pick the lure that the fish will come for," Bryan began.

For the next hour and a half they sat on the bank slowly filling their fish box. Sarah was surprised how quiet Bryan could be, and she thoroughly enjoyed this peaceful time in the young boy's company. She would most certainly accept if he should ask her again, for she had completely forgotten the inward calm this simple pastime could bring.

The following morning she returned to the manor and continued the search, but to her disappointment, the only thing she could find was a statement that a cousin was an heir presumptive and not an heir apparent because "legally the holder of a dignity, as long as he lives, may have a son to inherit."

It was the words "as long as he lives" that troubled her, for they seemed to mean that only if a son was born while his father was alive could he inherit, and this made her quite downcast.

"Well, do you find anything in those thick lawbooks that could be helpful?" Robert asked her, for he had come into the library twice while she had been studying them, and she had not realized there was anyone but herself in the room.

They were with Aunt Agatha, having a glass of sherry in the drawing room before supper, and Lady Pelham and the young people had not yet come down, so Sarah explained the only thing she had read so far that seemed to have any pertinence.

Robert looked serious, but to the surprise of the others, Lady Agatha spoke up.

"I distinctly recall, when I was just a young woman, that a newborn son whose papa had died some months before became an instant marquess," she told them firmly. "I'll look it up in my diaries when I get back upstairs, and you can then have someone check the records of that family."

"Are you sure, Aunt Agatha?" Sarah asked, for she could not quite believe that she had spent two days looking for something her aunt could have told her about in a trice.

"Of course I am," the old lady snapped. "At my age it's not the distant past that's difficult to remember. It's what happened yesterday that I forget."

As good as her word, the next morning, after having breakfasted as usual in her bedchamber, Aunt Agatha came downstairs clutching a thick but unmarked leather-bound journal.

"She doesn't look very well, Robert. Do you think that the excitement is too much for her?" Sarah asked.

"Perhaps a little," he said, "but if you had to live with Adele day in and day out, you might not look very well either, my girl."

Sarah frowned, for it had not occurred to her how difficult it must be for Aunt Agatha to live with their stepmama year after year, particularly when everyone was by now completely aware that there was nowhere else for her to go.

But now this would no longer be the case, for if she must have a companion she could think of no one else who would suit as well as Aunt Agatha.

"I have it right here, my dear," Lady Ramsbottom began. "It was almost fifty years ago, when the Marquess of Battersley died suddenly, leaving a wife and three daughters, but no son and heir. Lady Battersley was already quite obviously increasing when he died, and all would have gone to his younger brother if she'd had a girl, of course. There was much speculation and a lot of money won and lost in bets at White's and elsewhere when she gave birth to a boy,"she said, her face wrinkling into a smile at the recollection. "The poor boy inherited everything right away, but his uncles were appointed guardians and he could touch nothing until he came of age, and he was as closely guarded as the crown jewels."

"I'll bet he was," Robert said, "It's not a childhood I'd wish on any youngster of mine."

"Didn't his mama have any say in his upbringing?" Sarah asked in surprise.

Her aunt shook her head. "In my day women were not as outspoken as they are now, and there was nothing the poor thing could do, for the marquess had left his money in such a way that the uncles held the purse strings. Her daughters were a great comfort to her, of course, until marriages were arranged for them, and I believe she eventually went to live with a widowed sister in Bath. I remember seeing her there once when my Cedric took me to try the waters. Bath was a beautiful town in its heyday, you know. Much nicer than it is now," she rambled on, enjoying the opportunity to have an audience.

Sarah put an arm around her aunt and hugged her. "You're wonderful, Aunt Agatha," she said. "There I've been poring over those old lawbooks of Percy's for hours, and now all I have to do is send a note to Mr. Musgrave and have him look up the Battersley case."

Robert raised his eyebrow. "Do you mean to tell Jethro

about it when he gets back, or are you going to keep it to yourself for the time being?" he asked her, grinning.

She frowned, pursing her lips, then said, "That depends on his attitude when he returns. He was not exactly pleased when I made my announcement, was he? Just imagine, expecting I should have gone to him right away and told him, a complete stranger, that I thought I was increasing!"

"Don't think too badly of him, Sarah," her brother suggested gently. "He's put a lot of his time and effort into this place, you know, and it must have been quite a shock. I must admit that I wouldn't at all blame him if he went back home and waited there until he found out if it was a boy or a girl."

Sarah's eyes opened wide. "And leave the estates in the hands of that bailiff, Jim Bennett? He'll come back to an awful mess if he does that and then I have a daughter, for though I can do the bookwork, I could hardly ride the estates every day in my condition. And you've already put in more time here than you can afford."

Robert shrugged. "I've learned a lot too, for Percy had some darned good ideas that I plan to use at my own place. And, dash it all, Sarah, I like Jethro. He's a fine fellow, as you'll find out one of these days, and he doesn't deserve to have all this mess and confusion over an inheritance."

"You speak as though it's my fault, Rob," Sarah snapped. "It's just as confusing for me, you know."

Robert smiled knowingly, putting an arm around her shoulders and giving her a brotherly hug. "Try to see his point of view, will you? And don't gloat when he comes back."

"As if I would," Sarah said angrily, then slipped an arm through Lady Ramsbottom's. "Come along, Aunt Agatha, let's go through to the kitchen and see what Cook has in mind for dinner tonight."

Jethro was in the worst possible of tempers. He had arrived in London quite late at night and had gone at once to a small hotel he knew, for he wanted a change but had no wish to disturb any of his many relatives who were in town at this time of year.

The fact of the matter was, of course, that he was embarrassed that there were so many complications with his inheritance, and as he did not wish to have it turned into the latest *on-dit,* he preferred not to meet anyone who knew him well enough to ask questions.

The following morning he had visited his solicitor, described briefly what had happened, and had given him a full day to try to find out something of the matter. But when he went back the next morning, the fellow told him that he had been unable to find anything of any importance as yet, but he would keep looking for similar cases.

Jethro had then returned the morning after that, before leaving for the country, and told the man, who had represented him and his father for more than twenty years, that unless he found something pertinent to the matter and let him know within the next week, he would consider making a change in solicitors.

Without waiting for a response, he had stamped angrily out of the offices and across the street to where his old batman, who doubled these days as valet and general factotum, was waiting with the horses. Mounting swiftly, he set out at a fast pace for Mansfield Manor, leaving his man to jump quickly back, then mount and hasten after him.

10

"Don't you be such a spoilsport too, Sarah," Bryan said pettishly. "Jethro's back but he won't go fishing with me 'cause he says he's too busy, and you say that you just don't feel like fishing. I don't like it here anymore. I want to go home where there's always Billy and Tommy to play with me."

"Why don't you ask your mama or Meg to go fishing with you?" Sarah asked sarcastically, and immediately regretted it, for it wasn't her young brother's fault that she felt a trifle down-pin these days.

She put out a hand and ruffled his always unkempt brown hair. "Come with me to the village, for I have to get some fresh ribbon for a bonnet, and then when we get back, I'll join you at the stream," she said so persuasively that he looked a little sheepish.

"All right," he said, his voice gruff, "as long as you'll buy me some toffees as well."

"I'll buy you a whole bag full," she promised, laughing, "but don't blame me if you don't want any supper tonight."

There was little chance of this, however, for it seemed he had reached the age where there was no end to his appetite, and Sarah could have sworn he had grown an inch since he first arrived at the priory.

They went down a lane and through the fields, which was the quickest way to the village, Bryan running ahead and kicking at every stone or clump of grass that caught his eye while Sarah strode along enjoying the fresh air.

"What's the matter with Jethro? He's not been the same since he came back from London," Bryan said, taking giant backward strides so that he could face her as he spoke. "Did you do something to make him mad at you?"

She shook her head. "Not intentionally, and I'm sure he will realize that sooner or later. I do have something to tell him, though, and he's making it impossible by completely avoiding me. If you get the chance, you might let him know that I need to talk with him alone."

"I will," Bryan said solemnly, pleased to have something to do that sounded important.

When they reached the village, she had no trouble procuring the ribbon, for black was always in stock. Then she kept her word and brought a large bag of toffees for Bryan, extracting a promise, however, to save some for the next day or he might just succeed in making himself sick. Then, when they returned to the priory she sent him off to get the rods while she changed into a more serviceable gown.

They were sitting in a comfortable silence on the bank of the river, feeling an occasional nibble on their lines, when Bryan suddenly said, "You know I found out what's wrong with you, don't you?"

"I didn't know anything was wrong with me," Sarah said with a short laugh.

"Well, it's true that you're going to have a baby, isn't it?" he demanded.

"Yes," Sarah admitted, not sure she liked the direction he was leading, "but that's hardly something wrong."

"Then why is everybody so upset about it? And why do you want a baby when you're not married anymore? How do you get babies, anyway?" he asked, sounding almost belligerent.

Sarah sighed. "I can understand your wanting to know,

Bryan,'' she said gently, "and I think you're probably old enough now to understand a little, but it's not something a sister can talk to you about. Would you like me to ask Robert to explain it to you?''

His cheeks had gone quite pink with embarrassment, and he nodded, then fumbled with his rod and immediately got a strike. To Sarah's relief, by the time he had landed the trout he had forgotten all about his questions.

She did speak to Rob that evening, and he agreed to have a talk with his little brother the next day. With much relief, Sarah put it out of her mind, for one thing she always knew was that if Rob once said he would do something, it was as good as done.

All that was left now was for her to have her conversation with Jethro, but either Bryan had not seen him or Jethro did not care to discuss anything with her, for she did not meet him on her walks the next day, and she was quite disappointed.

She did, however, run into Sir Malcolm Howard in the village. When she came out of the draper's shop she heard his voice just behind her and swung around.

"Sarah, my dear, I do not see your coach. May I give you a ride?'' he asked, jumping down from his phaeton and determinedly taking the two small packages out of her arms.

"It's nice to see you, Malcolm," she murmured, "but I really don't need a ride, for I was quite enjoying the walk. How have you been?''

"Fine, as usual. Just got back from a week or so in London," he declared, then looked at her closely. "But I would feel even better if you did not walk the countryside without a maid or someone in attendance. Particularly if there is any truth in the rumors I've been hearing, or do you perhaps not wish to discuss it?''

"I don't at all mind talking about it to an old friend," Sarah replied, deliberately ignoring his first comment, "though the rumor went around much earlier than I could have wished, for servants do so enjoy to gossip. I am delighted, for as

you know, both of us always wanted children." She allowed
him to help her into the carriage as she spoke, for she knew
there was no gainsaying him once he was determined to give
her a ride.

"I must say that you look extremely lovely today," he
said softly, "but I heard also that Lady Pelham now means
to stay until the baby is born, and how you will tolerate that
woman for so long, I am really not quite sure."

Sarah laughed. "I keep thinking of things that might
persuade her to go home, but so far none has had quite the
right effect. I am, however, still hoping."

He steered the carriage to the side of the street as a lone
rider came toward them; then Sarah noticed that it was Jethro.
For some strange reason, she felt embarrassed that he had
seen her riding with Malcolm, and as he came closer, it was
obvious that he was far from pleased. Sir Malcolm, who had
slowed down and meant to stop the carriage altogether to
greet him, was quite taken aback when Jethro just raised his
whip in salute and rode by.

"How strange," he said to Sarah, frowning. "The new
earl seemed so very friendly when we met at the priory, yet
just now his expression was positively surly."

Sarah decided to say nothing about the inheritance to Sir
Malcolm for now, for no one except Aunt Agatha and Rob
knew very much about it, and it was really only hers and
Jethro's concern.

She shrugged lightly and changed the subject. "We had
a visit from Florence Kendal the other day," she told him.
"Adele did not like her at all, and I must admit that from
her appearance in unrelieved black one might have thought
that her husband had just died, not mine."

Sir Malcolm gave her a calculating look. "You are aware
that she was on the friendliest of terms with Percy before
he met you, are you not?"

With an amused smile Sarah said, "Of course. Percy made
sure I understood what his relationship with her had been,
and that it would never have led to marriage," she said softly.

"In the very gentlest way, he helped me grow up, you know, and by the time we had been married a half-year, there was nothing we could not discuss without embarrassment."

"That was the impression I got when I visited with you," Sir Malcolm said cautiously, "and at first I found it most disconcerting, I must admit. I'm not sure even now that I approve of it, but it was my friend's business and not mine. My own marriage was by no means so modern, shall we say, and my own dear wife would have been most surprised had I told her everything that I did."

Sarah's smile did not reveal her amazement at his admitted disapproval. She had always thought of him as a good friend of Percy's and, of course, a perfect gentleman, but now she could not help but wonder what kind of secrets he had kept from his wife. He had always made quite frequent trips to London. Did he perhaps have a ladyfriend there?

After his strange statement, it was somewhat of a relief to Sarah when they reached the priory, but she still felt obligated to ask him if he would like to come in for tea. Much to her relief, he declined, and after helping her down from the phaeton, he went on his way.

"I noticed Sir Malcolm brought you home," Lady Pelham remarked as Sarah passed her a cup of tea. "It's early, of course, but I do believe he is taking more than a casual interest in you. Don't forget, it would be foolish to make any promises until you've been to London."

Sarah laughed out loud. "You surely don't think I'll go to London with a baby to nurse, Adele. I'm afraid you'll have to do without my company in town next Season."

Her stepmama looked completely shocked. "You don't think to nurse the child yourself, do you? It's not at all the thing to do. You'll hire a wet nurse and a nanny and leave the child with them until it's old enough to do more than just cry and sleep."

As her stepmama spoke, Sarah suddenly realized how Adele had done that very thing with both Bryan and Meg.

They had scarcely seen their mama until they were walking and trying to talk.

She didn't even realize that she was slowly shaking her head until Adele again spoke up.

"You're not going to get out of it, you know, Sarah. Margaret needs your help in finding the most suitable husband, and I mean to . . ." She stopped sharply when she realized that Robert and Jethro had just walked in and were eyeing her curiously, then went on in a different tone, "Jethro, how nice to see you again. When did you get back from London?"

"A couple of days or so ago, my lady," the earl said smoothly as he walked over and took the place next to Sarah on the sofa. "I have, of course, been very busy since my return."

"I'm sure you must have been," Adele chattered on, "for Robert tells me that he will be going home next week."

As though by prearrangement, Robert took over and engaged his stepmama in conversation, leaving Jethro free to address Sarah.

"I imagined that your boyfriend would at least have come in for tea," he said softly, chuckling when she looked at him indignantly. "Did you perhaps scare him off with the same look you're giving me?"

"You did not look quite pleased with life yourself when you rode past us in the village," she said in sugary tones, forgetting that she had resolved, when next they met, to say nothing that could set his back up.

"A certain young man told me, after I returned from that ride, that you were anxious to have a word with me. Is that really true?" he asked.

"Yes, but not here," she murmured.

"Ah, an assignation with a beautiful young woman always appeals to my baser instincts. Do you have any suggestions for our rendezvous, or would you prefer to march directly into my study and beard the lion in his den?" His blue eyes were twinkling merrily. "I did put back all those heavy lawbooks you took out, by the way, for I needed a little room to work on my desk.''

Sarah couldn't help but laugh, for in this mood he was quite charming and she completely forgot how cross she had been with him for avoiding her. Then she flushed, for he was looking at her in a way that made her feel rather strange, but in a pleasant sort of way.

"I would like to have another cup of tea, Sarah.''

Lady Pelham's voice brough Sarah back to earth. She took the cup from Rob's hand and refilled it; then she noticed that Meg had come into the room.

"Would you like a cup of tea, Meg?'' she asked, ''or would you prefer a glass of milk?''

"I'm far too old to be drinking milk, Sarah,'' her sister said sharply, moving her chair close to Jethro's side of the sofa. ''I'll have tea and some of that Madeira cake. Isn't that your favorite, Jethro?''

"One of them, Meg,'' he agreed, then asked kindly, ''What have you been doing with yourself all day?''

"Nothing much. I meant to go to the village with Sarah, but she left earlier than I expected. Of course, I didn't know that she had arranged to meet Sir Malcolm there,'' she added slyly.

"You couldn't have known, for I had made no such arrangement,'' Sarah said sharply. ''In fact, had you accompanied me, he would not have found it necessary to bring me home. He apparently thinks it dangerous for ladies to wander around the countryside alone.''

"He's quite right,'' Lady Pelham asserted. ''In any case, so much exercise is not good for you in your condition. You should start having the carriage brought around.''

"You're not hesitating to use the coaches, are you?'' Jethro asked. ''You know they are there for your use also.''

Sarah shook her head and, noticing that her stepmama, had gone back to her conversation with Rob, said softly, ''She's quite wrong, you know. Exercise in moderation is very good for me. I feel far better after a good walk, and

I shall continue to walk for as long as I possibly can. I'll come up to the manor if you prefer it. When would be the best time?''

"Tomorrow morning? Whatever time you wish. Why don't you come to breakfast first? Mrs. Pennyfarthing would be delighted." He grinned engagingly.

"About eight o'clock, then?" she suggested, and he nodded.

Sarah saw the unhappy expression on Meg's face, and deliberately drew her into the conversation, though vowing to herself that she'd get Adele to leave and take this poor girl with her if it was the last thing she did. Once away from here, she was sure that Meg would quickly find new interests and forget all about this puppy love.

Mrs. Pennyfarthing was all smiles when Sarah came through the door with Jethro.

"How nice it is to see you, milady," she said, just as though she had not seen her less than a week ago. "Everything's ready. All your favorite foods. It's a real treat to see you again."

The breakfast room was exactly as it had always been, with Rivers standing by to fill up their plates and pour steaming cups of coffee. But once the food was in front of them, Jethro gave a nod, and the butler left, closing the door firmly behind him.

"Let's eat first," Jethro suggested, "and then we can talk over coffee, for you look as though your appetite has returned."

Sarah smiled gratefully, and as she ate, she made mental notes of some of the foods that might be served at the priory just for a change. She had been surprised, when she left the house earlier, to find Jethro propped against a tree waiting for her. He said he had been out and thought he might as well walk back with her, but she had a strong suspicion that he shared Sir Malcolm's views on her walking alone.

Whatever the reason, however, it had been nice to see him there, waiting for her with a smile on his face.

She took a sip of the fragrant coffee and made a firm resolution to have the cook at the priory take a few lessons; then she looked up to see Jethro watching her while he patted his mouth with his napkin and then sat back in the chair.

"Cook outdid herself," he remarked. "Just the mere mention of your name seems to work wonders with the service around here, and I seriously doubt that you've ever raised your voice to any of the servants."

"No, I've never needed to," Sarah agreed. "You see, I don't order them to do things, I ask, and it's surprising how much more eagerly they respond."

He nodded, then sat waiting for her to tell him why she wanted to speak with her.

"As you saw when you returned, I came over here and spent two full days going through those awful lawbooks. To go through every one would take months, I'm sure, but I did have every intention of returning the following day to continue my studies when I left them out like that." A faint flush tinged her cheeks, for she had not meant to leave his desk in such a way.

"They're too heavy for you to carry around anyway," he said firmly. "I was pleased, really, that you hadn't put them back."

"Anyway, I went back to the priory that afternoon earlier than usual, for Adele had sent Bryan over to get me. Apparently Lady Florence Kendal, one of Percy's old flames, had called and my stepmama disliked the woman on sight," she told him, with a quite mischievous grin.

The warmth of his smile seemed to give her the most heady feeling for a moment, but then she decided it was more likely to be just her imagination.

"When Florence had gone, Adele went up to rest, and I went fishing with Bryan, and when I got back, there were just Rob and Aunt Agatha there in the drawing room, so Rob asked me how I was getting along with the lawbooks. I wasn't making any progress, and said so; then suddenly Aunt Agatha told us she recalled a case when she was a young woman, where a newborn son became an instant marquess because his father had died several months before.''

Sarah was quite serious now, for she was sure that Jethro wasn't going to like what she had to say.

''I must admit that I waited most impatiently until the following morning, when Aunt Agatha brought down a diary from fifty years ago, and in it was the name of the family and the date the baby was born. The mother was quite obviously increasing when the marquess died, and everything would have gone to a younger brother of the marquess's if the child had been a girl. There were bets placed at White's and elsewhere, as you can imagine, on what the child would be.'' Her eyes were moist as she looked at Jethro. ''I'm afraid it's not the news you would like, Jethro, but it's better than waiting and wondering what the position is. I wrote at once to Mr. Musgrave, giving him the name—it was the Marquess of Battersley.''

Jethro got up and went over to Sarah, drawing a chair closer and putting an arm around her shoulders. ''Don't be so upset, my dear. It is better to know, or at least to be pretty sure. And it has started the two of us talking about it like normal people. I'll send a note to my own solicitor, and then we'll wait for them both to confirm it. But in the meantime, let's talk about the estates.''

''What do you mean?'' Sarah asked, puzzled.

''Your brother can't stay here much longer. We all know that, and though you can keep the books, you can't get around the property now, never mind in a month or two, can you?''

Sarah shook her head.

''Then let's do this. I will stay on, taking care of things as I intended, and if you have a girl, I will be the new earl. If you have a boy, I will remain Viscount Newsome, but I would like to be co-guardian of your child whether it's a

boy or a girl," he pronounced. "I believe Percy wished it
also. Would you mind that?"

She looked into his questioning eyes. "No, you must know
that I very much want you to be."

"Very well, until the baby is born, I will stay here, then,
but will take no monies for myself out of the estates except
to pay for the day-to-day running of the manor. If you have
a girl, everything will be mine anyway, but if you have a
boy, I'll still stay on until either you remarry or until he's
of an age to take his rightful place here. In that event, of
course, I would need to take some form of reimbursement
from the estates themselves, and I think we should not
even discuss amounts until such time as it becomes necessary."

Sarah breathed a huge sigh of relief. She felt as though
a weight had been taken from her shoulders. Jethro was going
to stay on, no matter what happened, and he no longer blamed
her for her condition. She turned toward him and felt tears
of relief course down her cheeks as he took her into his arms,
holding her close and murmuring reassuringly.

It lasted only a few moments, and he did not take advantage
of her in the slightest, but there was no doubt that their
relationship had undergone a subtle but quite definite change.

As she drew away, Sarah asked, "Would you mind if we
don't tell Adele anything for now? I'm still hoping she'll
leave of her own accord, and would like to give her a couple
of weeks to do so."

"Can Lady Ramsbottom be trusted not to tell her?" he
asked.

"Completely," Sarah said grinning. "She wants her to
leave more than I do."

He shook his head. "What an awful life that poor woman
must have led since she went to live with Lady Pelham,"
he said, "or was your father alive when she moved there?"

Sarah nodded. "Not only was my father alive, but he had
not even met Adele at that time. Aunt Agatha was widowed

and so she came to look after Robert and me, but then, just a couple of years later, Papa remarried. She stayed because there was nowhere else for her to go. And now, whatever happens, I mean to keep her with me.''

11

When Robert arrived a few minutes later to go over the day's plans with Jethro, he noticed something different about his sister, but made no comment, for he was pleased to see her looking completely at peace. He had left the priory with more of Adele's complaints ringing in his ears, and knew something would have to be done soon about their stepmama, but for now it was enough to see Sarah looking the way she always should.

She would not hear of either of them walking back with her, for it was now ten o'clock and time they got started with their work, she said. So Jethro reluctantly let her go while Robert watched the two of them with a great deal of interest.

It was a pity he had not warned Sarah of Lady Pelham's mood, for when she arrived back at the priory it was to find her stepmama in a fury.

"I insist that you inform the servants that they are to do what I tell them, Sarah," she said, almost screaming with rage.

"What is the matter, Adele?" Sarah asked, soothingly. "Who is disobeying you?"

"That girl of yours. I told her to come and fix my hair, for I heard you were already out and about, and she absolutely refused to do so,'' Lady Pelham snapped. ''She just turned her back on me and walked away.''

Sarah sighed. It had been such a wonderful morning until now.

''Betty works for me, as you very well know, Adele, and she had duties to perform for me even though I was not in the house. What was wrong with using the maid you have?'' she asked with most remarkable patience.

''She does not have quite the right touch with my hair, and I refuse to be insulted by a servant. If you had but a grain of proper feeling for me, you would send for Betty at once and reprimand her severely,'' Lady Pelham said angrily.

Sarah shook her head. ''I will question her about the matter, in private, and if I find that she was rude to you, I will reprimand her, but I have not yet heard what it was she said to you.''

''It wasn't what she said, it was her manner. She turned away while I was speaking to her. This is the very worst-run establishment I have ever had the misfortune to live in, for you spend most of your time going for walks instead of attending to your duties. When do you give the staff their orders? I've never yet seen you do so.''

''That's because you are not out of your bedchamber when I speak with them at eight o'clock in the morning, or even earlier sometimes,'' Sarah said mildly. ''But I would not like to feel that you are staying in a place you dislike so much, Adele, just to please me. I am perfectly healthy, reasonably happy for a recent widow, and Aunt Agatha is all the company I require at this time. You know, I am sure, that if I needed anything at all, Jethro would most certainly make sure I got it.''

''I know what my duty is,'' Lady Pelham said severely. ''Your papa would turn in his grave if he felt I was not taking care of you at a time like this. You were always inclined to be headstrong, and Agatha would be of no use at all in steering you in the right direction if you got one of those idiotic ideas into your head.''

Just as Sarah was about to ask what idiotic ideas Adele was speaking of, there was a knock on the door and George entered. "Excuse me, my lady," he said, "but there's a man delivering wines and I know you always like to inspect them.''

With a sigh of relief Sarah turned toward the door. "You must excuse me, Adele, for I have to attend to another of those duties. We'll continue our little talk later.''

She hurried to the kitchen, where she spent a full hour performing a task that required not more than ten minutes, and by the time she returned to the drawing room there was only a maid hurriedly dusting the furniture.

"Excuse me, milady," the girl said, curtsying prettily, "but Lady Pelham asked me to tell you that they 'ave gone to town and won't be back till this afternoon.''

"Thank you," Sarah said, giving her such a warm smile that the maid went back to her work with twice the energy she had shown before.

Lady Pelham heartily disliked taking Agatha with her on a shopping expedition, for the older lady heard only half of what she said to her, making a good gossip almost impossible. And it was no use taking her daughter, Margaret, with her, for the girl was as yet too young to enjoy such excursions. It would be a different matter altogether later, though, when their purpose would be to buy gowns for the girl to wear during her come-out.

As her mother, Adele was not unaware of the *tendre* the girl had for the earl, and the way she hung around the manor trying to get a glimpse of him or a word with him whenever she could. At worst, the girl would accomplish nothing and eventually get over it, but there was always the chance that he might find her a little interesting and leave himself open to a compromising situation. In that case, Lady Pelham would show no mercy, for Margaret would become a countess immediately, without all the expense involved in a Season in London.

And what a triumph it would be if her own daughter were the Countess of Mansfield and Sarah only the dowager, living in the priory. The chit would be glad enough to have her find her a rich husband if that were the case.

She was tired when they returned from the nearest small town, and rested all afternoon, so she did not see Sarah again until they were having their sherry before dinner. Robert was there by then, however, and keeping close to his sister's side in the most protective of ways, so she decided to wait until morning before bringing up once more with Sarah the question of insolent servants.

But when she was set on doing something, it always stayed in Lady Pelham's mind until her objective was achieved, and when she retired to her bedchamber that night it was on her mind to such an extent that it kept her awake. She looked around for the book she had been reading, then realized she must have left it in the drawing room. Of course, in a well-run household she would have been able to give a tug on the bellpull at any time of the day or night and get her maid up out of bed to fetch it for her, but here she knew she could ring forever and no one would come.

With a heavy sigh she got out of bed and lit her candle, then went quietly down the stairs to the drawing room.

At first, Sarah thought the screaming she heard had been part of a nightmare; then, as she awoke completely, she realized it was real and was coming from the hall outside her door. Quickly grabbing a robe, she wrapped it around herself and ran out of her bedchamber.

It was quite light, for a full moon was shining through the mullioned window at the end of the hall, and she could quite clearly see that the screaming was coming from Adele, who was slumped on the floor, completely beside herself with fear.

Bending down, Sarah put her arms around her stepmama and murmured soothingly, "It's all right, Adele, hush now, there's nothing to be frightened of."

"I saw him," Adele sobbed, "I saw the hooded monk just as clearly as I can see you now. It was horrible!"

"You think you saw the ghost?" Sarah asked in surprise, for she knew very well that Adele had never believed in things like apparitions.

"It was him, I know it was," Adele said hysterically. "They said he walked at full moon, and they were right."

Sarah looked up as Robert came out of his bedchamber in a burgundy robe and, almost at the same time, Bryan came out of his room in his nightshirt.

"What is it?" Robert asked. "Has she hurt herself?"

"She thinks she saw the ghost," Sarah said as quietly as she could, but Adele heard her.

"I know I saw the ghost." She was whimpering now and could not stop shaking despite the comfort of Sarah's arms. "He was standing over there with a long dark robe on, and inside the hood there was no face, just a black hole."

"Why did I have to sleep through something like that?" Bryan grumbled, then looked around excitedly. "Do you think he's still nearby?"

Robert had a lighted candle in his hand with which he lit al the wall sconces, both in the corridor and down the staircase, and then Sarah saw him slip quietly into Bryan's room. When he came out a few minutes later he looked at her and shook his head before silently opening Margaret's door and going inside. Once more he came out empty-handed.

"She's so sound asleep I hadn't the heart to wake her, and there's no sign of a hooded robe or anything in there," he murmured quietly to Sarah. He turned to Bryan. "Are you sure this was not one of your practical jokes, young man?"

"I was fast asleep until all that screaming woke me," Bryan protested, adding angrily, "but you always blame me, no matter what happens. I wish I had been awake, for I'd give anything to meet a real live ghost."

"A ghost wouldn't be alive," Robert said dryly, "and I'm still not too sure you weren't behind all of this. And what's more, if I find out you were, you won't get away with it this time. I'll personally give you the thrashing you deserve."

"Mama wouldn't let you lay a finger on me," Bryan answered sulkily, "but I'll show you all. I'm going to stay up tomorrow night and see if I can catch the monk—" Suddenly his eyes grew large with fear. "What was that?"

They had all turned as a knocking sounded on the front door; then Robert hurried down the stairs, pulled back the large bolts, and flung the door wide.

"What on earth is going on here?" Jethro asked. "I was taking a walk because I couldn't sleep, when I heard someone screaming and saw candles waving around."

"Come in, Jethro," Robert said, "and see if you can make heads or tails of the matter. It was Adele who was screaming, for she swears she saw the ghost of a monk in the upstairs hall." He added more quietly, "And don't convince her it wasn't, for this might be just the thing to get her to leave for home."

Jethro grinned widely, but he became serious again as he reached the floor above and watched as the pathetic figure of Lady Pelham, still shaking, was helped by Sarah into her bedchamber.

"Where did she see the apparition?" he asked.

Robert shrugged. "She says it was standing in the hall, wearing a long dark robe with a hood. She'd been down to the study to get her book, and it was so light that she had snuffed her candle as she got to the top of the stairs."

"I can assure you that no one left by the back of the house, for I was standing there, not twenty yards from the back door, when I heard the screams and then saw candles being carried about," Jethro assured them. "You didn't have anything to do with it, young man, did you?"

"That does it," Bryan snapped. "Every time anything happens, I get blamed for it. I'm going back to bed and I don't care if you never catch the ghost."

He went into his bedchamber and slammed the door behind him.

Jethro's eyebrows rose. "If it wasn't him, then who was it?" he asked. "Where are Margaret and Lady Ramsbottom? Not that I suspect either one of them, but those screams were loud enough to waken the dead."

"I went into Margaret's room, and she's hard and fast asleep—didn't even hear me come in," Robert said. "I would not, of course, think to enter Lady Ramsbottom's chamber in the middle of the night. Who knows, she might attack me with a poker, for she's a game old lady. She's also a deaf old lady when she wants to be, which might account for her absence."

Sarah slipped quietly out of Lady Pelham's chamber. "I doubt that she'll sleep for a while yet, but I mixed up a powder and watched her take it, so she'll get a little rest eventually. What were you doing out at this hour, Jethro?"

"Sarah," her brother scolded, "you can hardly expect Jethro to tell you about all of the assignations he arranges."

"Oh," she said, startled, for such a thing had never occurred to her. "I do beg your pardon."

Jethro chuckled. "I wish I could be so fortunate," he said, adding, "with the right lady, of course. I'm afraid it must have been that full moon riding high up there that made me restless. Anyway, I was having difficulty sleeping and did what I always used to on the Peninsula. I gave up trying to sleep, got up, and took a walk."

Sarah suddenly glanced down at the wrapper she was wearing, and at her bare feet. "Oh, dear," she said, "it was one thing running around like this with only Robert here, but I'd completely forgotten my state of undress. Do forgive me, Jethro."

Before he could say a word, she had turned and slipped inside her bedchamber.

"I don't know about you," Robert said, still laughing at his sister's embarrassment, "but I'm now wide-awake and would like to suggest going down to the study and having a nightcap.''

''A splendid idea,'' Jethro agreed, and the two men went quietly down the stairs and into the study, closing the door firmly behind them.

As soon as Sarah awoke the next morning, she went along the upper hallway to Adele's bedchamber and peered around the door to see if she was still sleeping.

''I'm not asleep,'' her stepmama said sharply, ''nor have I been for the last several hours. I have been lying here thinking about last night, and have most regretfully come to a definite conclusion. I cannot spend another night in a place where ghosts wander at will.''

''Oh, Adele.'' Sarah's voice held a note of remorse. ''Are you really sure that was what you saw? Could it not have been the deep shadows and the sway of a drapery or something that made you think it was someone moving?''

''I know what I saw, Sarah,'' Lady Pelham said grimly, ''and I think it would be best if you pack also and we'll all go back home. This is no place for a woman in your condition. Monks are probably quite averse to ladies who are enceinte, nd you never know what might happen.''

Sarah shook her head sadly. ''This is my home now, Adele, and I would want Percy's child to be born on his lands. I can't stop you going if you are determined to do so, but I feel that it would be quite wrong for me to come with you.''

It was the end of all Lady Pelham's careful planning, but there was nothing else she could do, for she had never been as frightened in all her life as she had been last night. If she spent another sleepless night here, she felt she would go completely and permanently mad.

''Do you know if Robert is abroad as yet?'' she asked.

''I'm sure he must be eating breakfast at this hour. Do you want me to find him and send him up to you?'' Sarah suggested helpfully.

"I would appreciate it, my dear, and send that maid in to me while you're about it, for she may as well get started on the packing. I'd like us to be on our way home directly after luncheon," she said firmly.

"If you like, I'll waken Meg and have my maid pack her things," Sarah murmured, "for your girl will have enough to do, I'm sure."

When Adele nodded, Sarah hurried out of the room, going first to tell Robert that Adele wanted to see him. "She's quite adamant about not spending another night under this roof, Rob, and I'm sure she'll want you to escort them."

He did not appear to be at all surprised. "Jethro and I talked about it last night after you went to bed." He grinned. "If you could only have seen your face when you realized how scantily you were dressed in front of Jethro. I'll swear you turned as red as a beetroot."

He dodged as Sarah aimed a blow at his head. "But we also came to the conclusion that I should take Adele back, if she wished to go, and then in about a month I'll return just to see how everything is going. I want to keep an eye on you," he ended more seriously. "What do you think really happened?"

"I have an idea, and I may know before very long. Ask me again before you go," she suggested.

"Margaret?" he asked.

She nodded. "I have to go now, for I want to get Betty doing her packing before she wakens and has time to hide anything."

She hurried out of the room and caught George as he was just hurrying toward the kitchens.

"Could you find Betty for me, George, and send her up to me in Miss Margaret's chamber," she asked, then went back up the stairs to her half-sister's room.

Margaret blinked as she saw who it was, for Sarah seldom if ever disturbed her in the morning.

"Mama has asked me to tell you that she wishes to leave for home, with you and Robert, just after luncheon today.

I know it's sudden, but you apparently slept through a most dreadful thing during the night,'' Sarah told her, noting that her sister's surprise was at the idea of leaving suddenly.

"I don't want to leave. I like it here,'' Margaret protested. "Why is she suddenly in such a hurry to go home?''

"She believes that last night she saw the ghost of the monk who is said to haunt this house at full moon,'' Sarah explained, "and she is adamant that she will not spend another night here.''

There was a knock on the door and Sarah answered it, stepping outside for a moment to talk to Betty and tell her that she was to pack for her sister and look specifically for anything that resembled a hooded cloak.

When she went back inside, she explained to Margaret, "My maid, Betty, is going to get your bags now and pack for you, so you'd best decide what you will wear for the journey.''

"I can't believe this. Last night I went to bed and everything was peaceful, and when I woke just now, everything is upside-down and we're going home at once. Did you have a quarrel with Mama?'' Margaret asked.

"Of course not.'' Sarah's voice was quiet. "I just told you that she saw the ghost last night, and is so terribly upset that she will not sleep under this roof again. I can't imagine how you could have slept through all that went on, for Mama screamed so loudly that it could be heard outside. Robert came in to see if you were all right, and you appeared to be in a deep sleep.''

"I took a long walk yesterday and was very tired when I went to bed,'' Margaret tried to explain. "What was Mama doing outside her room anyway?''

She didn't realize that she had given herself away, but Sarah caught it at once, deciding, however, to ignore it. "She went down to the study to get her book, for she was having trouble getting to sleep,'' she explained, then suggested, "Why don't you put on your robe and go and have a word with her?''

"I will," Margaret said, jumping out of bed. "Perhaps I'll be able to persuade her to stay a little longer. Come and help me, won't you?"

Sarah allowed herself to be taken back to Lady Pelham's chamber, passing Betty on the way. The maid had the valises in her arms and asked quickly, "Which gown did you mean to wear, miss?"

"Oh, the blue one. But you may want to wait until I get back, for I'm sure I can persuade Mama to stay a little longer," Margaret averred.

But despite her valiant efforts, Margaret was unable to persuade Lady Pelham to stay a single day longer, and after a completely exhausting morning spent trying to make sure that all their things were packed and loaded on the coach, Sarah sank into her chair at the luncheon table and reached for the glass of wine her brother had insisted she drink.

"Why do you have to do everything yourself?" he asked her. "You have a house full of servants, yet you run here and there without any regard for your condition."

She glanced at the extra place that had been set, and raised her eyebrows.

"Jethro insisted on joining us. I told him you had meant to ask him, so don't let me down," he warned, then asked, "Did you find anything?"

She nodded. "Betty found a dark cloak with a hood, thrust to the back of Margaret's wardrobe," she told him quietly. "I can only think that she was awake, saw Jethro down below taking his walk, and threw on the cloak to cover herself up while she ran out after him. The last person she would have expected to meet in the upper hall was, of course, Adele. Margaret probably thought she was hiding in the shadows and couldn't be seen. Then, when our stepmama started to scream, she slipped into her own chamber and pretended to be asleep."

"It's the best guess yet," Robert said.

"You don't think Jethro had anything to do with it, do

you?'' There was almost a note of pleading in Sarah's voice, though she was unaware of it.

"Decidedly not. But if Adele had not gone down for her book, and Meg had succeeded in meeting up with Jethro at that hour, it would have been a most compromising situation. He was very fortunate the whole thing happened as it did, or he would have sworn he'd been set up.'' Robert looked grim.

"I know, that's the other thing I was thinking of,'' Sarah said, "All I can say is that we have all been very, very lucky. But I'm going to miss you, Rob. You will write to me occasionally, won't you, and let me know ahead of time when you're coming back for a day or two?''

"Of course I will, you idiot,'' her brother told her. "And if you should need me, don't hesitate for a moment to send for me right away. I don't have to tell you to take care of yourself, do I?''

"No, you don't,'' Sarah said. "I promise I'll take very good care of both of us.''

12

Once Lady Pelham, Margaret, and Bryan had been helped into the carriage, and another half-dozen items added to the baggage loaded an hour ago, Robert took Sarah into his arms and gave her a firm brotherly hug.

"Now, don't forget," he told her, a worried frown on his face, "I'll be back for a day or two in about a month, but if you need anything in the meantime, just send a note in care of the Fergusons and they'll make sure I get it at once. Whatever you may think of Jethro, I know him to be a gentleman, considerate to a fault, and he'll not intentionally do aught to harm you, take my word upon it."

"I know, Rob," Sarah assured him. "We'll get along much better now, I promise. Just don't let Adele come back here on any pretext whatsoever, for I do believe I would dress up as a ghost myself to scare her away."

"Friar Tuck, perhaps?" he suggested, chuckling as he glanced down at the scarcely discernible bulge of her gown. "I still wonder if you planned it all, for I've never seen anything happen so conveniently. Now, just look after yourself and remember: take your maid with you if you feel like walking."

"I promise," Sarah said softly, "and if I didn't do so before, let me thank you now for everything you did for me.

I don't know what I would have done without you, Rob.''

"Nonsense," he said gruffly. "What are brothers for, anyway?"

Suddenly Lady Pelham's plaintive voice interrupted. "If we're going to get to the inn before nightfall, we'd best be off right away, Robert. I can't think why you two couldn't have done your leave-taking before now."

After another hug, and a kiss on his sister's cheek, Robert mounted and signaled for the coachman to move ahead. At the bend in the road he turned and waved to Sarah, who was still watching; then, once they were out of sight, she walked up the path and back into the priory.

"This is what is known as blessed quiet," Lady Ramsbottom remarked. "Do join me in a second cup of tea, Sarah, and we can enjoy listening to the silence."

Sarah had to laugh despite herself. "You know you're nothing but a fraud, Aunt Agatha, for you can hear as well as I can, I'm sure."

The old lady chuckled. "What's that you say, my dear?" she asked, holding a hand cupped behind her ear. "When you're my age you can pretend to be either deaf or eccentric or both, and get completely away with it, but don't you be in too much of a hurry to grow old, for you've a lot of life and happiness ahead of you yet.

"Now, tell me, Sarah. What really happened last night? I could hear the ridiculous screaming from Adele, and then all of you making enough noise to waken the dead, but I know the one thing that wasn't there was a ghost, no matter what that fool Adele says."

"She believes it, so that's all that matters," Sarah said with a laugh, delighted to know that her aunt's former, outspoken manner had resurfaced.

"It was Margaret, wasn't it?" Lady Ramsbottom asked. "I knew it must be, for she had been pretending to sleep through that awful racket."

"I think she must have been getting a little more desperate for Jethro's attention than we realized, saw him below, taking a walk, and decided to join him." Sarah gave a slight shrug. "Anyway, it really doesn't matter now. You and I can settle down to a nice comfortable existence here, and Meg will soon forget all about Jethro."

"Particularly without Adele egging her on," Lady Ramsbottom said dryly. "She would have liked nothing better than for Margaret to take your place here, and had no scruples about encouraging the girl's childish *tendre*. But that's behind us now, and I must say that I'm looking forward to your little one coming much more than I would have believed. I thought I was long past the time when I wanted the feel of a baby in my arms, but perhaps I'll change my mind when I hear it screaming. Which do you want it to be, a boy or a girl?"

Sarah sighed heavily. "For Percy's sake, I suppose I should want a boy, but for myself I'd really like a girl, I believe, and it would certainly make things easier for Jethro. He's worked so hard here that it doesn't seem fair if he has to give it all up."

"Now, don't you let that worry you for a moment," Lady Ramsbottom warned. "It's out of your hands completely, and it's not as if he would be left without anything, for he does have lands of his own, or so I understand."

"I know," Sarah said with a sigh, "but his brother looked after them all the time he was on the Peninsula, and it would probably make things extremely difficult if he had to go back and take them over from him now."

"You worry too much for your own good, my gal," Lady Ramsbottom said, adding with mock severity, "and isn't it time you went for that afternoon rest you promised Robert you'd take each day?"

Sarah's brows drew together in a heavy frown, though her eyes twinkled. "Oh, dear, are you going to be that sort of companion? I can see I'm not going to have the slightest chance to do anything at all for fear you'll write to Rob," she moaned. "Just don't try getting Jethro on your side, that's all, for sometimes he thinks he's still in the army giving orders to his men."

She was teasing, for their relationship had improved tremendously since that first night when she had stormed out of the library, and it continued to do so, while they awaited confirmation of their positions from the two solicitors.

At least once each week he sent his carriage to bring both ladies for supper with him, saying that he grew tired of dining alone, but it was quite obvious that it was Sarah's company he sought. She looked forward to those evenings far more than she would ever have admitted. He had flatly refused to allow her to send any of the servants back to the manor, and had actually added two more for additional protection.

Her days were surprisingly full, for she still took her long walks in the morning, but now a maid who had grown up in the village always accompanied her. It made the days more interesting for Sarah because her new companion was able to tell her things about the native trees and plants that she had not known before. Then, because there was no house-keeper as such at the priory, she took over those duties herself. There was always a decision to be made regarding what to have for meals, and supervision of the daily cleaning, for someone was bound to miss one of the chambers, or, much more frequently, the study.

She also started to catalog the pieces of furniture that had been there since the priory had been rebuilt some two hundred years ago. The desk in the study was one of them, its fine old wood lovingly polished to a rich glow, and there were a number of chairs that showed evidence of the meticulous workmanship of a master cabinetmaker.

Inevitably, her dislike of the priory began to diminish as she took a greater interest in its origins, and she soon realized that she no longer resented her move here from the manor.

From the day after her family left, Jethro had begun to stop by the priory at some time each day to make sure, he told the ladies facetiously, that they had no more problems with ghosts and such. Frequently his visits coincided with the appearance of the tea tray, causing Sarah to arrange for his favorite Madeira cake and scones to be served each day.

It was, of course, only to be expected that on one such visit he should find Lady Florence Kendal there, for she had become a quite frequent caller at the priory once she heard that he stopped in so often. The new earl did not socialize as yet, and this was, it seemed, her only chance of meeting him.

On this particular occasion, Sir Malcolm Howard was also paying a call, and it was he who asked, after the introductions had been performed, "Didn't you say that Lord Kendal had been killed in the wars, my lady? Perhaps the earl knew him?"

If it had been his intention to embarrass Lady Kendal, Sir Malcolm did not succeed. She had probably been asked that question many times before, and on this occasion she gave both gentlemen a sad smile and said, "My poor Charles was totally unsuited to warfare and was only out there at the instigation of his papa, who thought military service would 'make a man of him,' and frequently said so. He never attained any rank higher than captain, I'm afraid, and even that was too much for him, for he was not killed in a battle but on some sort of reconnaissance expedition."

"If he was sent out on reconnaissance, he was hardly lacking in courage, my lady," Jethro said sharply, "for it takes a very special person to go behind enemy lines and secure information. What unit was he with?"

"I really don't recall," Lady Kendal said weakly, "for I've tried to put it all behind me as much as I could since word came of his death. He spoke French extremely well, you know, which is probably why he was chosen, and I believe he was attached to several different units, but I can no longer remember any of them. You see, when we got married, he looked so handsome in his blue uniform, and I never thought for a moment, as the boat pulled away and he stood there waving, that I might not ever see him again."

She took out a kerchief and dabbed at her eyes, a gesture that effectively stopped any further questions.

"And how are you enjoying our lovely little corner of

England, my lord, now that you've had a chance to see more of it?'' Sir Malcolm asked jovially. ''I suppose you'll be hunting with us when you're settled down a bit more, eh? Favorite sport of the late earl, I can assure you, wasn't it, Sarah?''

He turned to look at his hostess, then suddenly realized the *faux pas* he had committed.

''Oh, my dear, I'm so sorry. It was Percy's favorite by far, but it can hardly be yours now, and I'll keep a tighter rein on my tongue in future, I promise,'' he said contritely.

Sarah, however, did not subject her guests to a second exhibition of grief in one afternoon, but merely smiled and said, ''It was never a sport I liked, Malcolm, for I have no wish to see animals killed for human enjoyment. Do you hunt, Jethro?''

''Not now,'' he told her grimly, ''and I may become most unpopular with the local hunt, for I don't care to see my crops ruined by a horde of men and women racing across them on horseback.'' He gave Sir Malcolm a rueful smile. ''You may not see my point of view, Sir Malcolm, for I don't believe you have land under cultivation, but it is a serious problem for many farmers.''

''A most dreadful sport, I must agree,'' Lady Kendal added with a rather unconvincing shudder. ''The only ladies you see taking part are the ones intent upon catching a husband by any means they can. Do you know that some of them actually ride astride?''

''I have no objection to women riding astride, for I believe a sidesaddle to be most dangerous if the horse should decide to go much faster than a slight trot,'' Jethro remarked. ''In fact, I have seen some riding habits where the skirt is divided so skillfully that you would not know it was for riding until the wearer actually mounted her horse.''

''How very interesting, my lord,'' Lady Kendal remarked. ''I understand that you are still a bachelor, and cannot help but wonder if you would feel the same about your own wife, if you had one, wearing something of that sort.''

Jethro smiled. "Yes, I am a bachelor," he agreed, "but as I have said, I consider sidesaddles dangerous. You surely do not think I would want my wife, if I had one, to put herself in danger?"

"That would depend upon your reason for marrying, would it not?" Lady Kendal countered slyly. "A sidesaddle might even be a means to an end, don't you think?"

His smile hardened somewhat and he shook his head. "As a soldier I have seen too much of war to ever invite it into my household, my lady," he said softly. "I can think of no reason strong enough for me to marry a shrew, and, in fact, I have no fancy at all at the moment to become a tenant-for-life."

Sir Malcolm, realizing that the conversation was getting a little outrageous for a drawing room, tried to change the subject.

"Have you reached a decision about keeping or selling some of the horses, Jethro? Percy had some fine hunters, as I recall, and I might be in the market if you did not wish to keep them," he suggested.

"I'm content to keep them in oats for now," Jethro said quietly, unwilling to reveal the tenuousness of his present situation, "and in any case, I would not sell anything of Percy's without first consulting with Sarah."

"Of course." Sir Malcolm nodded understandingly. "I would appreciate your letting me know, however, should you decide to sell."

"You'll be the first to know, Sir Malcolm," Jethro told him, "for I'm sure my cousin would have wanted you to have the first chance at them."

"I'd appreciate that," Sir Malcolm said; then he rose to leave, for though they were in the country, he still observed town rules of not overextending a visit. He glanced at Lady Kendal, for it would have been usual for a gentleman to offer his escort when they were going in the same direction, but that lady turned to look out of the window and appeared not to notice his departure.

The minute the door had closed behind him, however, she turned to Sarah and remarked, "You must find it terribly confining to live here after having a home the size and quality of Mansfield Manor, my dear. It's such a graceful, elegant home for a country house. I always loved it, but not as much, of course, as the house in Berkeley Square. Percy used to give such delightfully intimate parties there in the old days." She turned to Jethro. "You stayed there, of course, when you were in London last?"

He shook his head. "I haven't even looked at it as yet," he said. "I usually stay in the rooms I've always used in town when I'm there on business. To be honest, I'd forgotten all about it until you mentioned it."

"Would you like another cup of tea, Florence?" Sarah asked, "or a piece of cake?"

"Thank you, just a half-cup, if it's no trouble," Lady Kendal murmured, smiling her gratitude when Jethro got up to take the cup from Sarah and hand it to her. "And I believe I will have another small piece of cake."

Once again, Jethro did the honors, then resumed his seat, for he was waiting until she left to speak with Sarah alone. He had something to discuss with her privately, and had no intention of leaving until he had done so. Finally Lady Kendal had no option but to bring her prolonged visit to an end.

When she heard Florence's carriage finally pull away, Sarah felt suddenly tired and wished she could take a rest, but she realized why Jethro had waited and looked over at him with an unconsciously weary smile.

Lady Agatha rose. "I believe I'll have a rest before dinner," she murmured, motioning for Jethro to resume his seat, "and I hope you won't keep Sarah talking long, for she looks as though she could do with a rest also."

"My word on it, my lady," Jethro promised, holding the door for her. Then he closed it quietly and came back to where Sarah sat on the sofa and took her hand in his.

"I wanted to tell you," he said gently, "that I am sure my cousin's relationship with that woman, if indeed he had one, discontinued the moment he became betrothed to you. I knew him well enough to be certain that he would never have insulted you by continuing such an affair.''

''Actually, he told me of it before he brought me to the neighborhood, for he did not want any false rumors to reach my ears,'' Sarah said softly. ''I'm glad you told me, though, for I like to think that you held him in high esteem.''

He stroked the small white hand for a moment, marveling at its delicate strength, and wished, not for the first time, that the period of mourning was over. Then he could, despite his earlier statement, court her openly, competing, if necessary, with Sir Malcolm.

''You know, until Lady Kendal mentioned it, I had forgotten all about the house in town. Did the two of you spend much time there?'' Jethro asked.

Sarah shook her head. ''Not really. You see, I never had a come-out, so at first I was unsure how to go along, but Percy made a point of my being presented at court the first Season after we married. After that we would go into town and stay if we wished to see a play, or for some other such reason, but we never took part in the activities of the Season for more than a few days at a time.''

''You were, perhaps, fortunate, my dear, for I believe the London Season to be very much overrated. My mother has written to me that she may come up to town with her sister this Season, as a young cousin of mine is making her come-out. So I may be obliged to dance attendance on them at times, but in the normal way I would not wish to take part in it,'' he said, grinning.

To Sarah's complete embarrassment, she suddenly yawned, and Jethro laughed aloud, getting to his feet at once.

''It's all right. You don't have to drop me such delicate hints,'' he told her. ''You are dining with me this evening, aren't you?''

Sarah's cheeks were rosy as she nodded and allowed him to escort her to the door.

She took the stairs slowly, for Florence had tired her more

than she had expected, but she realized that, the introduction having been made, she would probably not see so much of that lady, for she would no doubt pursue Jethro quite openly from now on.

It was interesting, for she recalled quite clearly how Florence had tried similar tactics with Sir Malcolm. Sarah had often wondered what had passed between them to make them later so openly hostile toward each other. She would never know, of course, for she was sure that neither of them would talk about it to her, but she could hazard the guess that Florence had been holding out for marriage and that Sir Malcolm had had no such honorable intentions.

Betty was waiting for her in her bedchamber, with the covers turned back in readiness for her weary bones.

"You should have come up sooner, milady, before you got this tired," the maid scolded. "You can't hardly keep your eyes open."

"Well, just because they're closed, don't think to let me sleep too long," Sarah warned as she stepped out of her gown. "Lord Newsome's coach will be here at seven-thirty, and I don't want to keep him waiting."

"I'll have you ready long before that, milady," Betty assured her. "Just you have a nice nap now while I press the gown you decided on. Not that one black gown is any different from another, by my way of thinking."

Muttering to herself, she put the gown over her arm and left her mistress to recuperate from her tiring afternoon.

13

Dinner at the manor had been as enjoyable as usual for Sarah, who still loved the old house and had also grown to appreciate Jethro's company much more now that they no longer seemed to quarrel so much. Afterward, she and her aunt sipped tea while he visibly relaxed over a glass of brandy and a cigar. He was working hard these days, trying to bring about improvements on the estate that would benefit both the land and the tenants.

Soon Lady Ramsbottom's eyes began to close, and she slept comfortably while the other two spoke quietly of the changes put into effect, and then gradually got around to a discussion on some of the local people Jethro had met casually.

"I've had several invitations to dinner since I came here," he told Sarah, "and though I have so far declined them on the grounds of pressure of work, I know I cannot keep that up for too much longer. Were you and Percy on close terms with any of the locals?"

"He had a few old friends, Sir Malcolm being his closest, and in the wintertime we often entertained them, or went to their homes for dinner and cards or an occasional musical evening. They were all so much older than I that I never became very close with anyone except Lillian Lofthouse," she explained, "and you cannot have met her and her husband or you would have told me so, I am sure."

He smiled and his eyebrows rose a fraction. "I cannot help wondering why. Is there something different about them?"

"Yes, quite different. You see, they're cits, and proud of it, and Lillian is just about the best friend I have ever known."

There was a hint of defiance in her tone which quite intrigued Jethro. "You must tell me more about them than that," he begged.

She chuckled softly. "My stepmama met Lillian once, while she was at the priory, and was completely horrified. If I recall correctly, she told Aunt Agatha that she must discourage my acquaintance with such a dreadfully vulgar, encroaching woman or it would lower my standing in the neighborhood. Young Bryan adored her on sight, for she's tremendously large and deliberately wears the most outlandish clothes and jewelry. He was banished from the room, of course."

"And has she a heart of gold?" Jethro suggested. "She sounds wonderful, and now I can't wait to meet both her and her husband. Do they live nearby?"

"Yes, at Bedford Grange, a couple of miles or so north of here. You must have noticed it in the distance as you went back and forth to London, for it's quite difficult to miss," she told him.

"You don't mean that magnificent house set into the side of the hill, do you? It's one of the finest places for miles around and must have cost them a fortune. What was he in?" Jethro asked, now completely fascinated.

"Shipping was one of the things, I know, but he has a shrewd head for business and had a number of other interests according to Lillian, though she doesn't talk much about it. She's always too busy talking about her children and grandchildren, whom she adores. I believe Edward is her second wealthy husband."

They both turned to face Lady Ramsbottom as that lady

woke and added, "And she was quite ready to give you a piece of her mind, young man, when she thought you had thrown Sarah out of here."

"I hope you set her straight on that score," Jethro said with amusement, "for she sounds to be quite a character, and someone I should not like to offend. I'm not too sure about the other locals, but I suppose that I'll have to start socializing before long, though they must know by now that there's a chance I will never become the Earl of Mansfield."

He looked a little uncomfortable, and Sarah reached out a hand to touch his arm.

"I have discussed it with no one," she told him quietly, "but rumors always have a way of spreading around a small community like this one. You must be prepared to answer questions if you do decide to attend social functions, and I would really appreciate it if you would let me know what is being said in case I am placed in an awkward position."

He looked into the earnest gray eyes, and a distinct warmth came into his own as he stroked her soft cheek with one finger.

"You needn't worry, my dear. I'll keep in very close touch with you," he murmured.

The quite loud sound of Lady Ramsbottom clearing her throat interrupted them, and the old lady said, "I'm afraid that I'm having the greatest difficulty in keeping my eyes open. Do you think the two of you could continue this conversation in the morning?"

Jethro rose at once and tugged on the bellpull.

"My apologies, Lady Ramsbottom. Please allow me to escort you to the priory, for it is much later than I realized," he begged.

"There's no need for that," Lady Ramsbottom said gruffly. "I know you've got to be up early in the morning, and the coachman will see that no harm comes to us. I always enjoy dining here, and thank you again for your thoughtfulness."

Sarah put her arm through one of her Aunt Agatha's and

Jethro took the other as they walked slowly out to the carriage. Once they were seated, he stepped back and waved them off, then went slowly back into the house and through to the library, where he poured himself another glass of brandy and stretched out in the huge wing chair by the fire.

It was a good thing that the old lady had been along, he decided, for there was no doubt about it that he had wanted to kiss Sarah, and might very easily have done so had Lady Ramsbottom not made her presence known. And if that had happened, he would have been in a fine mess, for he did not want any woman to marry him simply because it was the most convenient way out of a difficult problem. He had waited long enough, and wanted a great deal more than that out of marriage.

But he wondered if she realized how tempting she was, for even with the child's presence becoming slowly more obvious, she was still the loveliest of creatures.

Perhaps it would be a good idea, he decided, to accept a few of those dinner invitations that kept appearing on the hall table. It might possibly be that he had let himself be thrown too much in Sarah's company for his own good.

Before he went to bed that night he determined to get out and meet some of the local people, and the following morning he selected a half-dozen of the invitations and sent notes of acceptance.

Three days later, by a quite remarkable coincidence, he ran into Lady Kendal as he rode through the village, and when she hailed him he had no option but to stop and greet her politely.

"How fortunate that I came into the village today, my lord, for you're the very person I wanted to see," she said, blinking up at him with her watery blue eyes. "You see, I only keep a carriage and pair since my dear husband's death, and this morning my groom informed me that one of the horses has gone lame."

Jethro was on horseback and could not for the life of him

think of why she was telling him. If she wanted a ride home, he was surely the wrong person to ask.

"I cannot think how I could be of service, my lady," he said, "if you need a ride home."

"Oh, no, you mistake me. I walked into the village, of course," she said with a short laugh, "but you see, I was invited to dinner this evening at the Hardacres', and a little bird told me that you were going to be there also. Would it be too much of an imposition to ask you to escort me there this evening? I would be most appreciative if you could see your way to doing so."

Jethro had not the slightest interest in taking the slightly faded blond woman anywhere, let alone to a dinner where people might get the wrong impression, but under the circumstances it would be quite churlish of him to refuse.

"Where and at what time should I call for you, my lady?" he asked courteously. "I believe the invitation was for six o'clock."

"Oh, yes, they keep country hours, of course," Lady Kendal murmured, giving him directions. "Would a quarter to six be all right?"

"Perfectly," Jethro said, "and now I'm afraid I must be on my way, for I am already late for an appointment. If you will excuse me?"

"Of course, my lord. It's so kind of you to oblige me in this way, and I do appreciate it," she murmured as she stepped back to allow him to leave.

Jethro did not feel at all kind, however, as his former batman helped him don suitable attire later that afternoon. Though he felt it was a ruse on Lady Kendal's part, he could not help but be curious as to her purpose and to wonder in what way she meant to be so appreciative.

"I'll need you to do something for me this evening," he told Bridges, when he was ready. "I'd like you to ride on the back of the coach, and when I stop to pick up a certain lady, I want you to go around to her stables and see if she has only two carriage horses, and if one of them is really lame.''

The batman grinned. ''Yes, sir,'' he said, giving his master a smart salute. ''Am I to wait for you or to make my way back here afterward?''

''There's no reason for you to wait. You can let me know when I return this evening,'' Jethro said. ''Of course, you realize I would prefer that the lady not know that she is being checked upon.''

''Of course, milord,'' Bridges said. ''Is there anything else?''

Jethro shook his head. ''Enjoy your evening. I understand that the Hooded Monk serves a good home brew.''

They left shortly afterward, and to Jethro's surprise, Lady Kendal was dressed and waiting for him when he reached her house. After helping her into the carriage, he resumed his own seat and within ten minutes they arrived at the home of Mr. and Mrs. Hardacre, a middle-aged couple with two well-behaved daughters in their mid-teens, and a son of twenty-one. Several other members of the local gentry had already arrived, and after partaking of a glass of sherry they went into the dining room, where twenty places had been set, with Jethro at his hostess's right hand as guest of honor, and Lady Kendal to the right of him.

''Are you enjoying our quiet little part of the country, my lord?'' Mrs. Hardacre asked when the first course had been served.

''Very much, ma'am,'' he told her. ''But you will appreciate, I am sure, that I have been very busy since I came back from Spain, and this is the first opportunity I've had to meet anyone other than Lady Wyndham's family.''

''Of course. How is dear Sarah getting along? It was such an awful shock, and her so very young,'' Mrs. Hardacre murmured.

''She's well,'' Jethro said, ''and looking forward to becoming a mother, as I am sure you must by now be aware.''

Mrs. Hardacre nodded. "Rumors of that sort spread very quickly in a small place like this, and though she's always been a little shy, there's no one I can think of who does not wish her well."

With the next course, Jethro was free to talk with Lady Kendal, and she took full advantage of it, chattering enough to give the impression that she had known him for months instead of a matter of days.

"Entertainment after dinner will be quite informal, I am sure, Jethro," she said, adding, "I hope you don't mind, but I feel as though I've known you forever, and I do hope you'll start calling me Florence."

"Of course," Jethro said a little gruffly.

"The two Hardacre daughters will probably give us a song or two after dinner," she went on brightly, "and perhaps some of the other guests will join in. I should think, with that lovely deep voice of yours, you might be similarly talented."

"Not at all, my lady," Jethro said quickly, quite horrified at the idea of being expected to entertain, for he had not been put in such a position since before he joined the army.

"It's such a pity that Sarah and Sir Malcolm could not be here, for they used to sing the most beautiful duets, just as if they'd been doing it all their lives," she went on. "Of course, Percy would never have believed anything underhand about either one of them—no matter what anyone said."

Jethro's eyebrows rose a fraction, but he made no response, and he deliberately ignored other similar hints she dropped as the evening progressed.

By the time it was over, he felt quite weary, for it had been a long day, and to her obvious disappointment, he declined Florence's offer of a nightcap when they reached her home. He was curious to find out if the lame horse was a ruse, and his valet quickly confirmed it when he came into his bedchamber a half-hour later to help him out of his clothes.

"There's a very nice mare for the lady to ride, milord,

and four carriage horses, all in the pink of condition,''
Bridges said with a grin.

"Thank you," Jethro said quietly, wondering if anything
Florence had told him that evening was true, particularly her
remarks about Sarah and Sir Malcolm. He had found that
people who dealt in lies often became so accustomed to it
that it became an effort for them to tell the truth.

To his relief, though he was constantly meeting Florence
at the homes to which he was invited, she used her own
carriage to go back and forth, and some of his hosts were
too anxious for him to meet their daughters to permit her
to monopolize his attention.

When he accepted an invitation to Bedford Grange, he had
not expected to see Sarah and her aunt there, for he knew
that she considered it wrong of her to socialize because of
both her mourning and her present condition. The Lofthouses
were good friends, however, and they had invited only Sir
Malcolm in addition to himself.

Despite Sarah's warning, Jethro found Mrs. Lofthouse to
be quite remarkable, both for her garish appearance in a low-
cut gown of purple and pink satin with a towering headdress
of fruit and feathers, and also for the unusual expression in
her eyes. There was nothing flirtatious about Lillian Lofthouse's eyes, but instead they looked at him in open, straight-
forward appraisal, and he found himself hoping he met with
her approval.

Neither could the hand she extended be considered dainty,
nor the jewels sparkling upon it discreet, and it seemed quite
natural that she took his own hand in a firm clasp. When
her eyes began to twinkle, he knew he had passed the test.

"Welcome to Bedford Grange, my lord," she said. "I
understand that between you and Agatha, my good friend
Sarah is in the best of hands. Keep it that way, and you'll
have no quarrel with me."

"I mean to, no matter what the outcome," Jethro found
himself telling her. "She's very special, and should not have
all these worries at such a time."

"She's strong and will come out of it all right," Mrs. Loft-house said with a nod. "She's going to have a fine, healthy little girl. I've predicted a lot of babies, and I've not been wrong yet."

Jethro found himself beaming, for of course that would be the easiest solution. Then he turned as a tall, thin man appeared at her elbow.

"Is this our new earl, Lillian? Why don't you introduce me, lass, instead of standing there gawking?" He thrust out his hand. "Real pleased to meet you, my lord," he said. "Sarah's told us quite a bit about you, and all good."

The handshake was firm, and the eyes shrewd, as Jethro had expected, but there was nothing gawdy about Edward Lofthouse's appearance. He wore a tight-fitting black velvet evening coat, pale gray knee breeches, and a silver brocade waistcoat, all undoubtedly by Weston of Old Bond Street. In the folds of his elegantly tied cravat nestled a large diamond pin, his only piece of jewelry.

"I'm delighted to be here," Jethro responded, "and I must admit I've admired this house and its location ever since I first saw it on the road from London."

"I'll give you a free tour of it after supper, if you like," Mr. Lofthouse offered, a glimmer of pride in his expression. "It's not often I look at something and know I have to have it no matter what, for I've never been one to throw money away, but that's what happened with this place. I just couldn't resist it."

Jethro nodded, for he meant to take him up on the offer of a tour; then Sir Malcolm came over to greet him quite cordially, if with a little more stiffness than his hosts. They had met frequently of late at the various homes to which both had been invited, and though they would never be the best of friends, they now rubbed along together quite well.

"Why didn't you tell me you were coming here?" Jethro asked Sarah when they were alone for a moment. "It would have been my pleasure to escort you, as you well know."

"After the trick that Florence tried to play on you, I

wouldn't have dared,'' Sarah said with a broad smile. ''And I understand that you were not at all taken in by the ruse.''

''Come, now, Sarah, I cut my eyeteeth too long ago to fall for something of that sort,'' he retorted, ''but this is different, for we are family and, after all, Lady Ramsbottom is with you. I'm curious as to how you heard about it, however.''

''In a village of this size the servants are all related to each other and they know about everything we do almost before it happens,'' she told him, much amused.

''Would you mind if I send one of our carriages back now,'' he asked, ''and we can then ride together, for there's no use in having two of them waiting.''

''But you may not want to leave at the same time as we do,'' Sarah protested halfheartedly.

''I would not think of letting you return to the priory without my escort,'' Jethro retorted, but his frown disappeared when she smiled and nodded her agreement.

A manservant entered with a tray of sherry as Jethro went to give the necessary instructions, and a little later they sat down to one of the finest meals he had ever been offered outside of London.

While the three ladies sipped their tea in the elegant drawing room, Edward Lofthouse showed the men around the gracious house that had once been the country seat of one of the most powerful and snobbish men in the land.

As though reading his thoughts, Edward Lofthouse remarked with a chuckle, ''You know, I've never held with ghosts and such, but you might think if there was any truth in it, there'd be a few of 'em walking these corridors of a night.''

Sir Malcolm shrugged. ''It came too easily to some of them, and they deserved to lose what they weren't prepared to lift a finger to keep, Edward. Now, I'm told that Jethro here puts in a longer workday than most of the men who work for him, and he doesn't even know if it will be his yet.''

"My wife says it will be," Edward Lofthouse said, "and it's not likely she's wrong."

"I'm used to working, and Sarah couldn't handle much more than the ledgers," Jethro said calmly, not wanting to enter into a discussion of the matter.

"If you were not here, she would without doubt have friends who would come to her rescue," Sir Malcolm put in quietly.

Jethro swung around. "But I am here," he said a little grimly, "so she has no need to be rescued."

Edward Lofthouse looked from one to the other for a moment, then suggested mildly, "I'm sure you'd both like to sample the brandy waiting for us in the study. The last shipment is so mellow it melts harsh words before they're even uttered."

He led the way, then proved to them that he had not exaggerated in his estimation of the brandy. A half-hour passed all too soon; then Edward Lofthouse led them to where the ladies sipped their tea. Soon it was time to take Sarah back to the priory before she fell asleep, for it seemed that, once more, she could scarcely keep her eyes open.

She did wake for a short time in the carriage, just long enough to thank Jethro for his courtesy and apologize for being such poor company.

14

To Jethro's considerable annoyance, it seemed that every time he called at the priory these days, Sir Malcolm was there, and on this particular occasion Florence was also seated, sipping tea and talking to Lady Ramsbottom.

He was of a mind to turn around and leave, but there was something he had been going to suggest to Sarah, so he waited until Sir Malcolm had left her side for a few moments and then said quietly, "I was wondering if you and Lady Ramsbottom might enjoy a day's outing to Tunbridge Wells later this week. I have some business to attend to there and I thought we might combine it with pleasure. You get away so rarely, and the ride would not be tiring for you both if we go in the landau."

"I say, what a splendid idea!" Sir Malcolm exclaimed, having returned the minute he saw Jethro approach Sarah. "I've been meaning to take a trip there for the last several weeks. Why don't we all go?"

"I would be most happy to join you," Florence spoke up, looking at Jethro rather than Sir Malcolm. "I know of a most delightful inn where we could stop for luncheon on the way. And if you two gentlemen are riding, I would rather do so also, and let the other ladies have the coach to themselves.

In your condition, you know, Sarah, you might even want to have a nap on the way back.''

Though Sarah's first reaction was indignation, she caught a glimpse of Jethro's look of frustration and she suddenly saw the funny side of the whole thing. They might just as well go, she decided, for it was quite possible that soon she might not feel like such a trip.

"What do you think, Aunt Agatha?" she asked, her eyes sparkling with fun. "If Lady Florence means to ride with the men, you'll surely not leave me alone in the carriage. We might even take that nap together. Besides, I've always wanted to try the medicinal springs at Tunbridge Wells, but Percy always contended that it was a lot of foolishness. And if we have time, we could go to Bayham Abbey and see if their ghosts can compare with ours.''

Although it had not been Jethro's intention to form a party, he could hardly tell the others so now, and he quickly suggested a day. He knew that Mrs. Pennyfarthing would make sure they had a well-stocked hamper with them in case Florence's inn should not materialize.

Soon a date was set for three days hence, and it was agreed that they would meet outside the Hooded Monk in the village. Sir Malcolm then made his excuses and departed, leaving Jethro frustrated but blaming himself for not having waited just a few minutes longer before suggesting the outing to Sarah.

The minute the door closed behind Sir Malcolm, Florence turned to Sarah and said archly, "I'm quite surprised, for I was sure Sir Malcolm would offer to ride in the carriage with you on Thursday, but of course Lady Ramsbottom will be with you.''

Sarah gave her a puzzled look, for she had not the slightest idea what she was talking about, but Jethro's sudden scowl was satisfaction enough for Florence. Her remark had not been in vain. Now she, too, was free to leave and let Jethro brood about what she had said.

Lady Ramsbottom got slowly to her feet when she heard

the front door close behind Florence. "If you young folks don't mind, I'll excuse myself also, for that gal has a way of tiring me out, and I feel much in need of a nap before I dress for dinner," she said, accepting Jethro's arm as far as the door but insisting she could manage with her cane from there.

He came back into the room and accepted the cup of tea Sarah poured for him, then sat down beside her on the sofa.

"Are you sure that the outing will not be too much for you, my dear?" he asked, having completely forgotten Florence's parting remark.

Sarah shook her head, looking quite amused. "I'm not an invalid, Jethro, and the change of scenery will no doubt be good for all of us. What time would you want to leave, for I recall you said you had business to take care of?"

"Would ten o'clock be all right?" he asked.

His left eyebrow quirked in the most engaging way, and Sarah felt an urge to reach out and smooth it, wishing she knew him well enough to do so without embarrassment. Instead, she merely nodded gravely, adding, "You said we'd meet at the Hooded Monk. Shall I send the others a note that we'll be there at ten?"

"I'd appreciate it if you would. How did you know that I hate to send notes?" he asked with a grin.

"It would seem that most men feel that way. At least Percy always did." She gave him a questioning glance. "You really didn't want to turn it into a party, did you?"

"No," he admitted. "To be honest, I'd much rather have you to myself. Sir Malcolm frequently behaves as though he has some sort of understanding with you, though I was given to believe that he was more a friend of Percy's."

"He was," she said quietly, "but he has been very kind to me since Percy died, and I am sure he is only trying to be helpful."

"Well, it can't be Florence he comes to see, for he appears to have taken a complete dislike of her and seldom speaks to her at all," Jethro pronounced emphatically. "I know, for I've seen quite a lot of both of them of late, since they have usually been invited to the gatherings I have attended. They avoid each other as though one of them had the plague."

"I'm not sure if we should rely on that inn Florence mentioned for luncheon. Do you think you should ask Mrs. Pennyfarthing to order a luncheon basket, just in case we cannot find the place?" Sarah asked.

"I was going to, for I had similar doubts, but perhaps you'd better take care of it, if you don't mind. You'll have a better idea than I of what to suggest she put into it. It may be wasted, but we'd best be on the safe side," he said, grinning. "You are supposed to be eating for two these days, aren't you?"

"Not quite, but I must admit that I do get hungrier before a meal now than I ever used to. I also tire more easily, which is nonsense, for I'm not doing nearly as much, but I think I'll join Aunt Agatha in a rest before supper."

She rose, then was ridiculously pleased as she felt the warm touch of his hand as he took her elbow to assist her.

It had rained quite heavily during the night, and when she fisrt awoke, Sarah feared that they might have to call off their trip to Tunbridge Wells. Eventually the sun peeped between the clouds, though, and by the time they were ready to leave, it shone brightly in a clear blue sky.

They were dressed and ready in good time, wearing bombazine carriage gowns that would be plenty warm enough if the day should become cool, as so often happened on an outing, and carrying muffs that served as additional pillows if necessary.

Sarah heard the carriage before she saw Jethro riding alongside, and by the time she and Lady Ramsbottom reached the front door he had dismounted and was waiting at the top of the steps to help them down and into the landau.

"You look very lovely this morning, my dear," he murmured for her ears alone as she followed her aunt inside.

She was grateful that Lady Ramsbottom was looking the other way and did not see how ridiculously pleased she felt at the compliment.

Lady Kendal and Sir Malcolm were mounted and waiting a little distance from each other outside the inn, and they both came over to greet Sarah and her aunt before the party, led by the riders, started out.

It was a perfect day, for the air felt clean and rain-washed, and it put them all in the best of spirits. Even Florence and Sir Malcolm appeared to have called a truce and were condescending to speak to each other on occasion.

Though it was a little tiresome for Sarah, she did not complain when Lady Ramsbottom nodded off, but watched the passing scenery. In fact, she had just estimated that they were about halfway there when Jethro called a halt and rode up to the carriage window, with Sir Malcolm just behind him.

"We're coming to an old bridge over a stream, but don't worry, there's plenty of room for the carriage," Jethro said. "I'll ride in front with Lady Kendal, and Sir Malcolm will bring up the rear."

Sarah was not at all alarmed, for it was certainly not the first bridge she had ever crossed by carriage, and she readily agreed, but Sir Malcolm started to argue about which of them should lead and which follow.

No one noticed as Florence rode over to look at the swiftly moving water, then gave a start as she read a sign posted on a stake a few feet from the bridge. With a swift movement she took her right foot out of its stirrup and kicked the sign over. There was a strange look of satisfaction on her face as she watched it fall onto a patch of wet grass and mud. She swung around to see if anyone had seen her, but found Sir Malcolm and Jethro busily arguing as to which of them should lead and which follow the landau.

Jethro had obviously won the argument, for he called to Florence to start over the bridge with him, just ahead of the coach, while Sir Malcolm stayed back to bring up the rear.

Taking it slowly and carefully, the coachman guided the

horses up and onto the bridge, behind the riders, and they had almost reached the middle when there came an ominous sound of wood creaking and then a loud crack as one of the supports gave way and the carriage tipped, then hung at a dangerous angle, throwing Sarah and her aunt sharply against one side.

"What has happened?" Lady Ramsbottom asked, her voice rising in alarm as she heard the sounds of the frightened horses.

"I'm not sure," Sarah said, "but I have a feeling that the bridge gave way. Try to stay as still as you can, Aunt Agatha, and I'm sure Jethro will come and get us out. Are you injured?"

"I don't think so, though I've no doubt these old bones will let me know soon enough," the old lady grunted. "What about you?"

"I fell on you, I'm afraid," Sarah told her, "and I'm not sure if I could get off even if I thought it wise."

"Sarah, are you all right?"

Jethro's voice sounded strange to her ears, and she wasn't sure exactly where he was, but she called back, "Yes, I think we're both all right. What happened?"

"The bridge gave way," came the terse response. "Don't move an inch if you can help it, while I work out a plan to get you out."

It seemed to Sarah that the waiting was interminable, and she became frightened, not for herself, but for the child she carried and for the old lady whose fragile bones had broken her own fall. What would happen to them if the rest of the bridge gave way and they fell into that cold, swollen stream? she asked herself.

The welcome sound of Jethro's voice interrupted her morbid thoughts.

"Don't worry if you feel the coach moving a little, Sarah. We're trying to secure it so that it can't fall any further, and then we'll bring you out through the door, if we can open it, or else the window. Are you still both all right?"

"Yes, I think we are, but please be as quick as you can."
She tried not to sound frightened, but knew that her voice
had a distinctly tremulous note.

"That's my girl. Just hang on and we'll have you out in
no time at all."

His voice sounded reassuring, and she could hear him now
giving orders as though he was back in the army, and it
seemed that there were men there obeying them.

Then the coach slipped and she gave a little scream before
realizing it had stopped moving.

"It's all right, Sarah. Don't worry. It won't be long now,"
Jethro called reassuringly.

To Sarah it felt like an hour since the bridge had given
way. In fact it was no more than fifteen minutes before the
carriage door was opened above her and Jethro's strong arms
lifted her up and carried her off the bridge, setting her down
on the bank of the stream before going back to see how Sir
Malcolm was handling the rescue of Lady Ramsbottom.

A motherly woman wearing a large apron came bustling
over with Florence and introduced herself as Mrs. Barnes,
the farmer's wife. She gave Sarah a glass of something that
looked most unpleasant and tasted even worse, and Sarah
set it down after the first sip.

"Drink it up," Florence told her sharply, but Sarah shook
her head.

"I don't need anything except a good cup of tea," Sarah
said decidedly. Muttering something about having told the
lady so, Mrs. Barnes hurried off, returning only a moment
later with a tea tray.

Sir Malcolm had not been so fortunate in his attempt to
rescue Lady Ramsbottom, however, as Jethro found when
he returned to the bridge. A rope had slipped and the carriage
had slid so that it was part in and part out of the fast-moving
stream. There was no immediate danger of the vehicle being
swept away, but Lady Ramsbottom was now sitting in a pool
of ice-cold water and must be got out at once before she took
a chill.

Between the two of them they eased the old lady through the opening and took her immediately to the farmhouse. There Mrs. Barnes helped her out of her wet things and, despite Lady Ramsbottom's protests, into one of her own flannel gowns, then insisted she have a wool blanket wrapped around her, and sat her in front of the kitchen fire.

The tea had been having a wonderfully soothing effect upon Sarah, for she had stopped shaking and was feeling almost back to normal, but when she saw her aunt being carried toward the farmhouse, she jumped up and followed behind as quickly as her shaking legs would permit.

Jethro stopped her at the door. "She was less fortunate than you, my dear, and got a bit of a soaking," he said. "Give them a few minutes to get her wet clothes off her and into something dry. There's a big fire in the grate and she'll be as warm as toast in no time at all."

"What happened?" she asked, alarmed.

"While I was bringing you over here, one of the ropes slipped and the far side of the carriage went into the water. She's a game old lady. She said she was all right, and told me it wasn't the first time she'd had a soaking and probably wouldn't be the last. How are you feeling?" he asked.

"I'm all right now, but I'd like to see for myself how Aunt Agatha is," she protested, and as the door opened then, she left him and slipped inside, going over to her aunt and giving her a worried look.

"You needn't look like that, my gal, for I'm all right except for a few bruises. And you don't look too bad yourself now. I believe we were very fortunate to get out of there alive, though," the old lady said. "I wonder if they'll be able to get the carriage out of the water."

"I don't know," Sarah said vehemently, "and I really don't care now that we're both safe. I imagine Jethro will work something out with the local people."

Once Lady Ramsbottom was feeling herself again, with her own dry shawl around her covering Mrs. Barnes's best

Sunday gown, the rest of the party came into the farmhouse to await the arrival of the hired carriage Jethro had sent for.

"I know it's too late to suggest it now," Sir Malcolm said to no one in particular, "but as all the locals seemed to know that the bridge was not safe, don't you think they might have put a sign up warning people?"

"Begging yer pardon, milord," Mrs. Barnes spoke up, "but there was a sign there. I saw it myself this morning, not ten minutes afore you people started to cross it, and there was no one came by before you did, for I can see the end of the bridge from my kitchen window."

Sir Malcolm shook his head. "I'd be willing to swear that there was no sign there when we crossed, for I started over here to get help, and remember quite clearly turning around to make sure the coach had not moved. There was no sign of any sort there then," he said firmly.

To satisfy himself, however, he went with one of the young farmhands to take a look, and when they came back the boy was carrying the sign, its message covered with the mud in which it had lain.

It was a mystery, and one destined not to be solved, though at least two of the party, Florence and Sir Malcolm, knew or had a good idea of what had happened.

When Jethro appeared in the doorway, he paused, his eyes searching the room for Sarah; then he saw her and went over, the picnic basket in his hands.

"If this good lady has no objections," he said, smiling at Mrs. Barnes, who positively beamed back at him, "I believe we should try to eat a little of this, for it will be some time yet before the carriage gets here and we are able to leave."

Sarah had thought she would not be able to eat a single bite, but with Jethro at her side, encouraging her, she found herself enjoying the slices of cold chicken, ham, and hard-boiled eggs washed down with a glass of vintage wine.

They had almost finished when Jethro excused himself, for he heard the sound of a carriage outside. All was in order, and ten minutes later they thanked the farmer and his wife and entered the hired carriage. Though it had a musty smell, and was certainly not as well-upholstered as the landau had been, neither Sarah nor her aunt made any complaint, for they were simply glad to be starting for home at last.

Jethro wanted Florence to ride in the carriage with them, but she made it more than clear that she would rather not, and neither Sarah nor Lady Ramsbottom felt the need of her company. Despite the hard seats, both ladies fell fast asleep and woke only when they reached the Hooded Monk. Sir Malcolm, who had said nothing of his suspicions to anyone, came to say good-bye, but Florence merely waved from a distance, then cantered up the lane toward her home.

When the carriage pulled in at the priory, Jethro was immediately at the door offering an arm to each of the ladies. Their early return was unexpected, but more wood was thrown on the drawing-room fire at once and a tea tray followed within moments.

"I'll not stay long," Jethro said, "for I know that you must both be feeling quite exhausted after such a dreadful experience. I must tell you, however, that I cannot for the life of me think of any two ladies of my acquaintance who would have gone through such an ordeal without at least throwing a fit of hysterics."

"Rubbish!" Lady Ramsbottom said bluntly. "A lot of good hysterics would have done! I'm too old to start, and Sarah's always been of a more practical nature. I didn't get much chance to thank you for your help, my lord, but I most certainly do now. I really don't know how you managed to get us out without more than a mild soaking."

It had not been easy, particularly after the carriage slipped, and his worst fear had been that they and the carriage might be swept away in that fast-moving water, but he had no wish to give them more of a fright than they had already known.

"I believe I'm going to lie down for a while, however, just as soon as I finish this cup of tea," Lady Ramsbottom went on. "Excitement seems to wear me out these days."

"And how about you, Sarah?" Jethro asked softly. "Are you really all right?"

"Now I am," she said, "but I must confess that I was very frightened until I heard your voice."

"And then?"

"Then I knew that you would get us out somehow, for you must have come across much worse predicaments in Spain," she said seriously.

"Much worse," he agreed solemnly, but his eyes were twinkling and his mouth quivered with suppressed laughter now that it was all over with apparently no harm done.

"How dare you laugh at me, Jethro!" she said, trying unsuccessfully to be cross with him, but she failed miserably and soon the pair of them were laughing together from sheer relief.

When they were serious once more, he took her small hands in his and told her simply, "I was more scared than I've ever been in my life, for it was difficult to secure those ropes, and the slightest movement could have toppled the carriage completely over and carried you both downstream."

"If it had, you'd have rescued us somehow, I'm sure," she said airily, while stifling a yawn. "That farmer's wife was so good with Aunt Agatha, and I must admit that her tea was the best I've ever tasted in my life."

"And you may not know it, but your eyes are almost closing," he said gently, "so I'm going to leave you to get a good rest and, if you don't mind, I'll come back this evening to make sure you're both still feeling all right."

She nodded in agreement and allowed him to escort her to the foot of the stairs, but she did not see the look of tenderness in his eyes as he watched her climb slowly up them, then turn along the corridor and out of his sight.

15

Jethro stopped at the priory that evening on his way to a neighbor's home for dinner and found that both ladies had decided to eat supper in their rooms and have an early night. Sarah had left word for him, however, that he must not worry, for they were both perfectly well, but just a little tired.

Satisfied, he continued on his way to the home of a wealthy middle-aged widow, Lady Chisholm, who still had her youngest, unmarried son, Christopher, living with her and taking care of her small unentailed estate on the verbal promise that it would be left to him when she passed on.

Jethro had met the young man on a number of occasions and found him to be good company and an excellent card player, so it promised to be a pleasant, if not exactly exciting, evening.

After the events of the day, it had been his hope that he might not see either Florence Kendal or Sir Malcolm tonight, but just as he took a glass of sherry from the tray a footman held, there came a familiar teasing voice in his ear.

"What a long time it's been, my lord," Florence said mockingly. "Did you put your two charges to bed and tuck them in before making your escape?"

"Physically, no," he murmured, "but the ladies had a

most frightening and exhausting day, and I understand that they are dining in their rooms this evening.''

Florence nodded understandingly. "I was teasing, as you well know, Jethro. They were most fortunate you were there, for I cannot imagine anyone as well-suited as you to perform such a rescue.''

Jethro shrugged, reluctant to discuss the matter further, then looked around at the seven or eight people already gathered in the elegantly furnished drawing room.

"I believe that Sir Malcolm accepted, but he'll more likely spend the evening trying to get back into his lady's good graces for not performing the rescue himself today,'' she murmured.

"Now, just a moment, Florence," Jethro started to say angrily, but she put a finger to his lips.

"Not here,'' she whispered. "You surely don't want to be the one to give away their little secret. I'll most likely be at the opposite end of the table from you at dinner, but I'm sure we'll have a chance to talk later.''

Her words had, however, ruined the evening for him, and for once he even lost at cards, for he found it impossible to give them his usual concentration. He felt nothing but relief when the game ended and he was able to thank his host and hostess for their hospitality, bid them a good-night, and send for his carriage. The air felt clean and cool, and he regretted that it was not possible to stroll home as he had so often done in London after an occasional frustrating night at the tables.

When his carriage came around, he nodded to the coachman and stepped inside, then found, to his amazement, that he was not alone. Florence Kendal was sitting at ease in the opposite corner, with a satisfied smile on her face. He silently swore, and promised himself that the coachman would pay dearly for this.

"I do beg your pardon, my lord, but you were so engrossed in your game that I did not dare interrupt you and ask for a ride home,'' she murmured, fluttering her eyelashes and leaning toward him.

"Which of your four carriage horses is lame this time?" Jethro asked a little grimly.

Her laughter rang out so loudly that he could not help but wonder if she had imbibed a little too much of their host's excellent wine.

"So you made inquiries?" she said, amusement still lingering in her voice. "How naughty of you. This time, however, my horses were all fit and well but my coachman was not, so I told him to go home and to bed, for I knew that someone would be happy to see that I did the same."

The double meaning was not lost on Jethro, but he deliberately chose to ignore it. The last thing he wanted was an entanglement with a local woman, but this might be an opportunity to find out just what she was insinuating about Sarah and Sir Malcolm.

He came straight to the point.

"Your remark earlier this evening has been puzzling me. Have I perhaps missed something with regard to the relationship between Lady Wyndham and Sir Malcolm?" he asked bluntly.

"Sarah has always been very discreet, so I'm not at all surprised you noticed nothing, but we've all known each other for what seems an age, you know. At one time the four of us went everywhere together, though I've never cared much for Sir Malcolm myself," she said with a meaningful smile.

Jethro scowled. Such conduct did not seem at all like the widow he had grown fond of, but why should Florence lie about it? What had she to gain?

"And isn't it interesting how Percy's first wife was said to be barren, and so was Sarah, until just recently. Of course, most men will simply not believe that it is they and not their wives who cannot produce children. What do you think will be said if the baby has blond hair?" she asked suggestively.

"Nothing at all, I should think, for it is a well-known fact that many brown-haired people were fair-haired as children," he countered with some asperity.

"We know that, of course, but will the rest of the village?" Florence asked mockingly.

There was now no question but that Florence had imbibed more than usual, for even though the carriage had stopped outside her home, she remained seated, a rather foolish smile on her face, waiting for Jethro to make the next move. With a look of disgust he jumped down and handed her from the carriage, and she stood there swaying slightly.

"I have an excellent French brandy if you would care to sample it," she suggested, watching his scowling face with considerable amusement.

"So have I, at Mansfield Manor," Jethro said curtly. "I'll wish you a good-night, my lady. I may not see you for some time, as I mean to go to London in the morning."

"A sudden decision, my lord?" she asked, a note of glee in her voice for having obviously succeeded in perturbing him.

"A visit long overdue," he snapped, then climbed back into the carriage and gave the order to leave.

"Sarah's such a dear girl, and I promise to take good care of her while you're away," she called, then turned to walk a little unsteadily toward her front door.

She was aware that she had gone a little too far, but the champagne she and the son of the house had shared earlier, while his mama was still dressing, had been drunk too quickly and had gone to her head. She was not at all dissatisfied by the way the evening had ended, but she hoped Jethro would not stay too long in London, for she would miss him.

Jethro, however, looked far from happy as he drove away. He was disappointed in himself for having made such a grave misjudgment of Sarah Wyndham's character. He had liked her from the moment he first saw her, and he readily admitted to himself that his feelings had slowly changed into something much more than just liking. This evening had, however, been only too enlightening.

Despite her earlier indulgence, Florence Kendal had not

actually come out and said that Percy Wyndham had been cuckolded, but there had been no doubt as to her meaning, and he could not help but wonder if she would have watched her tongue more carefully had she been sober. Deep down, he still found such a thing difficult to believe, but he had seen for himself that Sir Malcolm was quite infatuated with Sarah.

When he reached the manor he recalled the excellent brandy he had mentioned, and decided it might help clear his head.

It did, of course, have the opposite effect, and an hour later, completely beside himself at the idea of Sir Malcolm's bastard son being put in his own rightful place, he went up to his chamber and told Bridges that they would be leaving the next morning for an indefinite stay in London.

Sarah had been up and about for some time, though her aunt was not yet risen, when George came to tell her that Lord Newsome was here and asking to see her alone.

"I have shown him into the drawing room, my lady," he told her, adding, "and I took the liberty of offering him a glass of sherry."

Sarah glanced quickly at the man, for it was not very long after breakfast—a little early in the day for sherry.

Yesterday she and Jethro had parted on the friendliest of terms, so it came as quite a disappointment when she saw his grim countenance. The smile on her own face faded to a look of concern. George was probably right to give him sherry, she decided, for Jethro's eyes did look a little bloodshot and his face a trifle pale.

He took the hand she offered and bowed low over it, but when he lifted his head there was a sardonic gleam in his eye that she did not care for at all. She allowed him to seat her comfortably, then waited impatiently to find out what was troubling him.

"You appear little the worse for your narrow escape

yesterday, my lady," he murmured, eyeing her slowly from head to toe in a rather insulting way. "Did you have a restful evening?"

"I slept reasonably well, if that's what you mean, my lord," Sarah snapped, "and it appears that I suffered no serious injury other than a few bruises."

"And Lady Ramsbottom, did she sleep well, or did she perhaps need a sedative to make sure she . . . got her rest?" he inquired.

"If you must know, Jethro, she did take something to help her sleep, for she was a little more shaken than she at first appeared," she told him. "I have not yet seen her myself this morning, but I understand she is feeling much better and will be up and about in a little while. I will be sure to let her know that you were concerned about her."

"Thank you, I wish you would," he said smoothly. "As I will be leaving for London within the hour, I will not be able to speak to her myself."

Sarah looked up at him curiously. "It seems rather sudden, for I don't recall your saying anything yesterday. Has there been some new development to cause you to rush off so quickly?"

His chuckle held little amusement. "You might say so, my lady." His voice was so quiet now that she had to listen carefully to catch what he was saying. "Someone who knew Percy very well indeed suggested that it might have been his fault that he was unable to have sons."

She waited for him to continue, not at first understanding his meaning at all, but aware that he was looking at her in the oddest way.

"The person you spoke to believes that I will bear a daughter, then?" she asked quite innocently. "If you recall, my friend Lillian was quite convinced also that it will be a girl."

He shook his head. "That was not exactly the person's meaning, my dear," he said bleakly. "The implication was that he could not produce children at all."

She looked puzzled at first, for after the warm way he had spoken to her yesterday afternoon, she had not expected such a change in his manner. Then the full realization of his meaning came to her.

"And you believed this? You've known me now for almost four months and you think that I am the sort of woman who would c-cuckold her husband?" She was so very shocked that she found it difficult to get the words out.

"I notice you haven't denied it," Jethro said, and there was a sadness in his voice, but by now Sarah was too angry to notice.

"Nor will I. You may think what you choose." She was suddenly furious with him. "Go to London, and see what your fancy, expensive solicitor thinks. If you try to assert that my child is other than Percy's, I'll fight you through the courts and right to the House of Lords if I have to."

She was completely unaware that she had placed her hands on her swollen body in an instinctively protective gesture, but Jethro noticed.

He bowed low with exaggerated civility, so that she did not see the pain in his eyes; then long strides took him to the drawing-room door, and though he closed it quietly enough behind him, Sarah jumped as she heard the outer door slam so loudly that it seemed to shake the rafters of the old priory.

Completely oblivious of George's startled face, she ran out of the room and up the stairs to her chamber, unable to see for the tears that came unheeded. She had started to love Jethro in a way that she had never loved Percy, and had thought he felt the same way, so that the pain he had inflicted had gone very deep. She was quite convinced that it would never go away.

When, several hours later, she still would not allow her personal maid, Betty, into the chamber, and refused to come down to luncheon, the latter went to see Lady Ramsbottom, who was not feeling quite her usual self after the previous day's accident, and had partaken of a light nuncheon in her chamber.

"Now, start again, my girl, and this time tell me slowly what you believe happened to cause your mistress to be so upset," the old lady said gruffly.

"It was George, milady, who told me, for she got up feeling as fine as fivepence, or as near as could be expected, and ate a real good breakfast, according to Cook. She was in the kitchen giving orders for luncheon and dinner when his lordship arrived, and real poorly he looked, according to George, who said he must have been badly disguised last night.

"The door was closed, so there's no knowing what went on between them, but suddenly it opened and shut quick-like, and his lordship was through the front door, slamming it fit to wake the dead."

"Mm," Lady Ramsbottom said, "I believe I heard that and wondered what it was. Then what happened?"

"George came to fetch me, and he said her ladyship had come running out of the drawing room and up the stairs as though the devil himself were after her, and that tears were pouring down her face."

"I went up right away, of course, but she wouldn't let me in. She just called for me to go away and leave her alone, and though it's quiet in there now, she still won't let me near her."

Easing herself carefully out of her chair, for as she had feared, the events of the previous day had taken their toll on her old bones, Lady Ramsbottom went to Sarah's bedroom door and knocked sharply. "Sarah, I'm worried about you and I want to see if you're all right. Come to the door, if you please," she called.

"I'm quite all right, Aunt Agatha. I'm just resting. Please go away and leave me alone."

The voice was so different from her niece's usual lively tones that Lady Ramsbottom forgot her own hurts and became alarmed. She turned and went slowly back to her bedchamber, Betty following closely behind her.

"I want you to order the coach brought around for me in five minutes, Betty. I'm going over to Mansfield Manor to speak to Jethro Newsome and find out from him what happened," she said determinedly.

But when the old lady arrived at the manor, it was to find that Jethro had left more than an hour ago for London, and no one could tell her how long he might be gone.

"Do you know where Bedford Grange is, young man?" she asked the coachman as she returned to the carriage.

"Yes, milady," he said with a nod. "Are you going to pay a call?"

"Certainly I am. Take me there at once."

It was a sudden idea that had come to her, for Lillian Lofthouse appeared to be Sarah's best friend, and she knew she could rely on her discretion. But when she reached the beautiful country home, she hesitated, wondering if she was doing the right thing.

The decision was taken out of her hands, however, for suddenly a large figure in a bright green gown burst through the handsome front door and hastened to the coach. She looked a little taken aback when she saw only Lady Ramsbottom inside, but she put out a hand to help her down and then escorted her into the house.

"We'll go into my sitting room, my lady," Mrs. Lofthouse said quietly, "for I have a feeling something is very wrong. And you don't look at all well yourself, if you don't mind my saying so."

"I'm all right, still a bit shaken up after a slight accident yesterday, that's all," Lady Ramsbottom said gruffly. "It's my niece I'm worried about."

Tea was brought almost at once, and as they sipped the delicious brew, the two ladies had a most interesting conversation, at the conclusion of which Mrs. Lofthouse hurried upstairs to change into outdoor clothes and accompany Lady Ramsbottom back to the priory.

Once there, Betty was sent for, and confirmed that nothing had changed since her ladyship had left.

"I know which is Sarah's chamber, and I'm going up to her right away. I'll get the door open, or I'll know the reason why," Lillian Lofthouse said grimly, "and when next I see Lord Newsome, he'll get a piece of my mind he won't forget for a long time."

She insisted on going upstairs alone, and when her sharp rap on the door was answered by the words "Go away," she said sharply, "Open this door at once, Sarah. No matter what is wrong with you, there is a little one to think of, and I promise you I'll have the door broken down if you don't let me in."

"Are you alone, Lillian?" Sarah asked wearily.

"Yes, I am. Your aunt is waiting downstairs," was the reply.

There was the sound of a key turning in the lock and the door opened slowly to reveal Sarah's pale, unhappy face. She stepped back to allow her friend to enter.

Mrs. Lofthouse closed the door behind her and turned the key once more. Then she put an arm around Sarah and held her in a comforting embrace.

"Come along, love," she said gruffly. "Let's sit down by the window and you can tell me all about it. You'll make yourself sick, and the baby too, if you go on like this."

"It was awful, Lillian," Sarah said. "Someone told him the baby wasn't Percy's, and he believed it." She hiccuped slightly as the last word came out.

"He did, did he?" Mrs. Lofthouse said grimly. "I wonder who it was put that idea in his head—as if I didn't already know. But why did you get so upset? You know it's not true."

"Because he actually believed I could do something like

that," Sarah said, still unable to understand. Then she smiled faintly. "But I told him that I'd fight him all the way if he tried to stop my child inheriting."

"That's the spirit, my girl," Mrs. Lofthouse said. "Youj must not let him treat you so shabbily and get away with it. You know who will be right behind you, I'm sure. Now, tell me what all the tears are about. Are you in love with him?"

"How did you know?" Sarah asked in surprise.

The rolls of flesh shook as Mrs. Lofthouse laughed at herself. "I wasn't always like this, you know," she said, her bright eyes twinkling. "I was once as young and slim as you, though never as pretty. But I'd my share of boyfriends until I met Horace and fell in love with him."

"Was he your first husband?" Sarah asked, forgetting her own problems for the first time in several hours.

Mrs. Lofthouse nodded. "That's right, but it wasn't all plain sailing for us, either. It never is, you know, if it's worthwhile. We had our ups and downs before we settled to getting married. The trouble is that Percy was more like a father to you. You've never been in love before, have you?"

Sarah shook her head.

"If he's the right one, and I have a feeling he is, then it will work out eventually, I promise. But now you've got to think about that little one. You've missed luncheon, I know, and that's not good. Shall I have a bit of something sent up for you now, and then we can see about making you look more like yourself?"

"Yes, please, Lillian. And thank you for coming," Sarah murmured, feeling a little embarrassed now at causing so much trouble.

"Isn't that what friends are for," Mrs. Lofthouse asked, "to help each other when they're needed?"

She gave a tug on the bellpull, then went to the door to tell Betty that her mistress would have a late lunch now. Then she stayed with her while she ate a satisfying meal, after which Betty combed her hair and bathed her face.

When she finally appeared downstairs, and apologized to her Aunt Agatha for worrying her so, no one would have known there had ever been any upset.

"And now, if you ladies will excuse me," Lady Ramsbottom said, "I believe I'll have a little rest myself, for all this gadding about is a little too much for me at my age."

Sarah was immediately contrite. "I'm sorry, Aunt Agatha, are you really sure you're all right? I didn't mean to put you to so much trouble."

"I'll do very nicely as long as I have a bit of rest," the old lady told her, touching her niece's cheek with a gentle finger. "Don't you start worrying about me now. Just take care of yourself for a change."

16

Jethro was in the lowest of spirits when he set out for London, for he had not meant to accuse Sarah of anything, but was most desirous of hearing her deny that her child could be that of anyone but Percy. He realized that her refusal to do so was perfectly understandable, under the circumstances, however, and that if it came to believing her or Florence, there was simply no doubt about whom he would trust, for he already knew Florence to be a liar and a cheat.

He was driving Percy's phaeton, and the fresh air felt so good on his face that his spirits inevitably improved and he began to enjoy the drive despite the fact that he knew he had done something quite unforgivable.

It was more than clear that Sir Malcolm was most interested in Sarah, but Jethro could not, for the life of him, imagine Percy involved in the kind of foursome Florence hinted at. And if that was untrue, then the rest of her ramblings were highly questionable, to say the least.

He was of half a mind to turn around and go back, and he did start to rein in the horses; then he decided it was already too late and the damage had been done. It would be far better to continue to London and stay there until he could

177

bring back a satisfactory answer from his own solicitor or Mr. Musgrave.

Despite his quite honest contrition, he could not help smiling at the way Sarah had looked when she was not concealing her feelings behind a polite facade. When really angry, she had been particularly striking, and he had most certainly deserved her wrath. He hoped, however, that he had not hurt her feelings too much by his lack of trust, and that he would be able to repair the damage when he returned.

He took it easy on the drive, resting both himself and the horses frequently, and reached London just after nightfall, staying once more at the lodging he'd always used when in the city.

The following morning he went to see his own family's solicitor.

"I'm afraid the news is not quite as good as I would have liked, my lord," the young man who came out to greet him said, taking him through to the office the head of the firm had always used. "My father is unfortunately somewhat incapacitated at the moment, but he explained to me the research he had done, and it appears that there have indeed been a number of precedents set."

Jethro already knew what the outcome would be, and while waiting for the young man to get to the point, he found himself noticing how very much like his father the fellow had become. He watched him sit down and lean both elbows on the desk, then place his chin on his clasped fingers in precisely the way the older man used to, and wondered if he himself had unconsciously adopted any of his own father's mannerisms.

"There has to be an official ruling on it, of course, but there is little doubt that you, as heir presumptive, will have to wait until the sex of the earl's child is known. If it is a girl, then you will inherit the title and entailed property, of course. Should it be a boy, however, the child will most decidedly become the new Earl of Mansfield, and you will remain the heir presumptive until such time . . ."

The voice droned on and on, while Jethro only half-listened, for he was wondering how he was going to make his peace with Sarah after behaving like such a sapskull the previous day. It would not be easy.

" . . . and we would recommend that until the outcome is decided by the birth of a child to Lady Wyndham, you remove yourself either to your own estates or to London. Under the circumstances, Lady Wyndham should remain in residence at Mansfield Manor and bear her child there. However, either you or a trusted representative must be present at the birthing to ensure that no substitutions are made."

The last sentence brought Jethro up short.

"Under no circumstances is Lady Wyndham to be subjected to such an indignity," he thundered, "and I'll not have it even suggested either to her or to her solicitor."

The young man looked askance, but after a moment he seemed to realize that his client would brook no argument, so he shrugged and said, "As you wish, my lord."

"As for taking up residence in town, I can think of nothing more foolish than to let estates that I have worked hard these last months to improve, now go to ruination. By all means, Lady Wyndham must move into Mansfield Manor and I must move out, but I can do just as well at the old priory," he said brusquely.

"Though I must say it is not what my father would have approved of, I can see that you are adamant, my lord, so there would be little purpose served by discussing either point further," the young man said quietly. "I will, of course, be at your service should you decide to follow our advice."

"I would not count on it, were I you," Jethro told him, getting to his feet. "Give your father my regards, and tell him I hope he's soon back on his feet again."

To Jethro's amusement, he was escorted out of the offices in a hurt silence; then he tossed a coin to the lad who had been holding the horses' heads, climbed into the phaeton, and took the reins.

His next visit was to old Mr. Musgrave, who had been the late earl's solicitor, and here, of course, the first thought was for Lady Wyndham.

After shaking hands with him, Mr. Musgrave showed him into a private office, then confessed that he had not yet written to let Lady Wyndham know his findings.

"However," he told Jethro, "we now know that there is no question about it. If she has a son, he will inherit everything, and she must have the finest care during her confinement. I mean to recommend a London doctor for the actual birthing, unless she is already consulting one from the city, for the greatest of care must be taken."

Jethro looked puzzled for a moment, then said, "I really do not recall anything being said about a doctor, but I will most certainly speak to her about it when I get back."

"You intend to remain at Mansfield Manor, then?" Mr. Musgrave asked.

"Probably in the priory," Jethro told him, "for Lady Wyndham cannot possibly take care of things there during the next few months. I have some business in town for a day or so, and then I mean to go back until after the child is born."

"Of course, my lord," Mr. Musgrave said, nodding. "Her ladyship informed me that everything is in the best possible condition, and that her aunt is staying with her to give her countenance. I hope the lady is not too old to be of help if anything should happen."

"I will personally make sure that Lady Wyndham has the finest care," Jethro said quietly, "and though I may have to persuade her to see a doctor, you may be sure she will do so."

Jethro's purpose in calling had been to ensure that both solicitors were in agreement, and having done so, he took his leave of Mr. Musgrave, promising to keep in close touch.

He had not meant to stay more than a couple of days in London, but the more he thought about that last dreadful scene, which neither of them was likely to forget very soon, the less anxious he was to face Sarah until some of her anger had faded. In any case, he told himself, he had not stayed in London for any length of time since he first went out to Spain, and an extra few days, visiting his club and looking up old acquaintances, might be most pleasant.

First, however, he decided to call upon his mother, who had written to tell him that she was staying in town with her sister to help bring out a young cousin of his.

He arrived at the house as the three ladies were just about to sit down to luncheon, and was shown in at once and another place set at the table.

"You'll have a glass of wine while Cook augments the simple nuncheon she had prepared, Jethro?" Lady Newsome suggested. "You are a naughty boy not to let us know that you were in town."

He had little or no appetite, but would not have disappointed his mama and aunt for the world, so he took his seat without demur, then turned to his young niece.

"What a lovely young lady you grew to be, Josie," he said gently, noting how a flush came to her cheeks at the compliment. "Have you been to any balls yet?"

She shook her head. "We got here only a week ago, and we've done nothing but visit the modiste, mantua maker, haberdasher, and dozens of other shops since we arrived."

"Do you have plans for this afternoon?" he asked, addressing his question to all of the ladies.

"We meant to pay some overdue calls," his Aunt Bridget told him.

"Must Josie go with you, or may I take her for a drive in the park this afternoon in my phaeton?" he inquired.

The girl's whole face lit up, and Jethro realized that if only she started to enjoy the Season, and smile more, she might take very well indeed.

"But of course you may," her mama said readily. "She'd much rather do that, I'm sure, than sit drinking tea with a lot of older ladies, wouldn't you, my love?"

Josie nodded, then gave him a mischievous grin. "You

don't happen to have your uniform with you, do you?''

He laughed. ''I'm afraid not. Do you fear that everyone will mistake me for your papa?''

''Of course not,'' she protested. ''But it always seems that men look twice as handsome in uniform. What time should I be ready?''

''Whatever time your mama and aunt are starting out,'' he said. ''I took care of my business this morning, and now have the whole afternoon frcc.''

Over luncheon they talked of town and the plans afoot for Josie's come-out party. Jethro gave his word that he would be there and wrote down the date so that he would not forget.

When the other two went upstairs to change, Lady Newsome stayed behind to find out more about her son's activities, for though he had written frequently, she had not seen him since he first went to Spain.

''It's such a comfort to know that you're no longer in danger, son,'' she said quietly. ''When you were fighting out there I had a terrible dread of something happening to you, though I tried my best not to let you know how worried I was.''

''I knew you must have been, Mama,'' Jethro told her, then added, ''but I'm not yet out of it altogether, for Wellington gave me a leave of absence rather than have me buy out. I had no idea what I was coming back to, you see, and as a matter of fact, I still don't know what the position is.''

Lady Newsome gave him a puzzled look. ''How do you mean? You did inherit from Percy, didn't you?''

He shook his head. ''Not yet, I'm afraid, and there's an even chance that I won't.''

He went on to explain the problem to her, and when he finished, she looked at him long and hard.

''Are you in love with Percy's widow?'' she asked shrewdly.

They had always been honest with each other, and there was no reason not to tell her the truth, but Jethro still hesitated a moment before replying. "Yes, I believe I am," he said quietly.

"You're not sure?" she asked.

"I wasn't until a few days ago, and now I find that she's in my every thought. It might be because I said something quite awful to her before I left for London, something unforgivable that, once said, cannot be taken back, and I almost dread returning, in case the wrong I did cannot be righted."

"If she loves you she'll forgive you, but she might make you suffer a little first," his mother said, smiling to herself. "At least, that's what I would do."

"You and Papa had occasional disagreements, but you didn't quarrel the way we did," Jethro told her, frowning at the recollection.

"We did when we were younger," Lady Newsome told him, "before we really settled down. Then, instead of being just in love, we found that a stronger, deeper love had grown in its place, encompassing both ourselves and our children. I cannot wish anything better for you than that, Jethro."

"You still miss him, don't you?" he said, reaching to grasp her hand.

She nodded. "There are all kinds of silly little things that happen and trigger a memory, but I've learned to be happy about them instead of sad, for they bring him closer. But enough of that. Tell me about Kent. Is it good rich land for grazing and farming?"

"Very good," Jethro said with a smile, "and much prettier than the north. The weather is surprisingly milder also. You'll have to come and visit if I ever get to stay there."

"You will," she said, smiling, "and I will come and see what kind of a young lady it took to make you settle down after all your travels."

There was the sound of light footsteps hurrying down the stairs, and Lady Newsome said, "Here comes Josie now. She's a nice little thing, a little lacking in confidence as yet, but with good manners, and I do hope she takes this Season."

"If I see any of the patronesses of Almack's in the park,

I promise to stop and speak with them," he said, his eyes twinkling at the thought.

"Do so, by all means," Lady Newsome told him, "for it will give the gal consequence just to be seen with you, I'm sure. I was hoping I might be able to persuade you to join us some evening if you're going to be here a few days."

"As long as you don't mean me to spend the whole evening with you, I'll be delighted to escort you more than once if it will help," he said agreeably.

"How long did Jethro say he would be in town, Sarah?" Lady Ramsbottom asked. "I only ask because that Jim Bennett was here asking about him."

"I'm sorry I didn't know he'd called," Sarah said, "for there may be something serious that needs a decision. Jethro said he had no idea how long he'd be gone, so I think I'll send word to Bennctt and at least find out what might be worrying him."

"You'd best tell him when to come or he'll call again when you're taking your nap, and I won't hear of your being disturbed. You need all the rest you can get from now on," Lady Ramsbottom said, her voice more gruff than usual, for she was trying to hide a decidedly sore throat.

She had begun to assert herself a little and make sure Sarah did all the things a lady in her condition should, instead of behaving as though nothing had changed. And Lady Ramsbottom also meant to give Jethro a severe scold when he returned.

Sarah smiled, for she had realized what was happening and did not mind at all, for her aunt was a very gentle bully. "I'll let him know, Aunt Agatha," she told her, "and now I think it must be time for tea, for I feel just a little hungry."

She started to get up to ring the bell, but her aunt was there before she had eased herself off the couch. "Now, look here, Aunt Agatha," she said with mock severity, "you'd best not indulge me so much or you might find that I turn into one of those women who spend the rest of their days having others wait on them hand and foot.''

"There's little danger of that,'' the older lady asserted, "and it will do me no harm to move around a little more.''

There was the sound of a carriage outside, and Sarah frowned and said, "I was hoping the two of us could have a quiet tea alone. Who do you think it can be?''

There was no need to guess, however, for the voice of Florence Kendal could be heard in the hall, and this time Sarah groaned. "Don't leave me alone with her, whatever you do,'' she whispered to her aunt.

"Oh, dear, am I too early? I could have sworn you'd be drinking tea by this time,'' Lady Kendal said loudly as she was shown into the drawing room. "Now, don't get up, Sarah, or perhaps you should, for I'd swear you've gained two pounds since I saw you a day or so ago.''

Sarah intentionally kept a blank expression on her face, then said sweetly, "I really didn't like to say so, Florence, but I was just thinking the same thing about you—and you have no excuse, have you?''

Lady Kendal looked down at her gown, a pale blue sarcenet with three rows of frills at the hemline. "It's this gown,'' she said, frowning and twitching the skirt. "I told the modiste that it was unbecoming, and tomorrow I'm going to take it back.''

"In the meantime, won't you take a seat?'' Lady Ramsbottom requested. "Tea has already been ordered and will be here directly.''

"I know it's too soon for you to have heard from the earl,'' Florence said. "He did, of course, stop by and let me know he would be gone.''

Though Sarah was almost sure it was a lie, the slight possibility that it was not still hurt.

"It's such a pity that you're not yet out of mourning, for his presence has so enlivened the social scene here lately,'' she said as she took a cup of tea from Lady Ramsbottom.

"We have become such good friends these past weeks, and he even suggested I might take a look at Mansfield Manor while he's gone and see what changes I might like to make."

There was a triumphant gleam in her eyes, and Sarah had gone quite pale, despite her determination not to let Florence see how upset she was.

Lady Ramsbottom's husky voice broke the tension. "If you're trying to pretend that young man has been making any promises to you, I for one don't believe it," she said bluntly. "All you're doing is attempting to make mischief, as you did there at the bridge, and I'll warn you that mischief-makers usually come off the worse for it in the end."

At the mention of the bridge, Lady Kendal gave a little gasp and the whole cupful of hot tea tipped onto her blue gown. She jumped up as Lady Ramsbottom reached for the bellpull.

"How dare you say such things to me," Lady Kendal said shrilly. "I had nothing to do with that sign, and you can't prove that I had. I'm leaving right now, and I'll tell everyone of the dreadful accusations you made."

George came in then, just in time to show her ladyship out of the room.

Once she had gone, Lady Ramsbottom looked at her niece in amazement. "I was not referring to the sign at all," she said. "You don't think . . . ? She couldn't have . . . ?"

Sarah sighed. "She may have done something, for she was near the bridge alone before we started over. But it can never be proved, so the least said, the best." She gave her aunt a worried glance. "But I don't very much like the sound of your voice, Aunt Agatha. You've been getting huskier as the day goes along. Are you sure you're not suffering a delayed reaction to that dunking?"

"I hope not," the old lady said, "but perhaps I will have a lie-down in a while and see if Jennie can bring me some honey to ease my throat."

"Oh, Aunt Agatha, why didn't you say something before now?" Sarah asked crossly. "I'm going through to the kitchen at once to have something made up for you, and I'll send Jennie right up with it. I thought you might be doing a little too well after that awful accident.''

As she hurried from the room, Lady Ramsbottom gave a sigh, then got slowly to her feet and went up the stairs, holding the handrail tightly, for she was beginning to feel decidedly unsteady on her feet.

The honey did little to ease Lady Ramsbottom's throat, however, and before nightfall it was clear that she had succumbed to much more than a cold. After sending an urgent message to Dr. Unwin, the doctor who had attended Percy, Sarah called for water and cloths and bathed her aunt's forehead in an attempt to reduce the fever that seemed to be raging through the old lady.

When Dr. Unwin came, he showed grave concern and gave Sarah detailed instructions on what should be done to try to pull the old lady through.

''There must be some reliable staff here who can look after her,'' he said quite bluntly to Sarah, ''for you should not be doing so in your condition.''

But though Jennie, Betty, and two more of the maids took turns in looking after the old lady, Sarah did not feel she could trust any of them entirely, and spent most of her waking hours in her aunt's small bedchamber.

17

I t seemed much more than a week since Jethro had left Mansfield Manor, but he did not regret his trip to London in the slightest. He had not realized how much he had missed his mother's sound common sense, and a visit with her had been long overdue. And Josie, his young cousin about to make her come-out, had blossomed delightfully under the attention she had received and now promised to be one of the most popular young ladies this Season. He doubted very much that she would become an Incomparable, but she would certainly be successful enough to be able to pick and choose where a husband was concerned.

There was now just one person he meant to see before he presented himself to Sarah, and that was Sir Malcolm Howard, the man who had been quite open about his interest in his best friend's widow. As soon as he reached the Manor, Jethro washed off the dust of the road and changed, for he meant to pay a call on Sir Malcolm and find out his version of the foursomes to which Florence had referred. He had little doubt but that the story was the product of that lady's very fertile imagination, but felt it would be as well to make doubly sure.

He had not been home more than a quarter of an hour, however, before Jim Bennett, Percy's bailiff, arrived and asked to have a word with him. A few minutes here or there wouldn't make much difference, Jethro decided, and told Rivers to show him into the library.

It was late afternoon, and no doubt the man had been home and had a pint of beer before coming here, but it was no excuse for the attitude he encountered in the bailiff when he joined him a few minutes later.

" 'Afternoon, milord, I 'eard you'd got 'ome and I just thought I'd stop by and find out who my boss is around here," Bennett said belligerently.

"Oh," Jethro said, disliking the man's attitude and waiting to see how far he would go.

"Aye. I came lookin' for you a couple o' times this last week, an' then asked at t'priory when you'd be back. 'Er ladyship sent word that she wanted to know what I was worryin' about."

"And did you tell her?"

"I did no such thing," Bennett said. "I told 'er, I'm either workin' for 'im or workin' for you, but I don't take orders from two at t'same time."

"You did?" Jethro asked, his voice dangerously quiet. "You actually said that to her?"

"Aye, that's what I told 'er."

"Well, now, I'll tell you something, Jim," Jethro said sternly. "You can vacate the cottage tomorrow, get all of your things out, and when I'm satisfied that you've earned it while I've been gone, I'll give you your final pay tomorrow night. Then I never want you to set foot on this land again."

Bennett looked as though he could not believe his ears. "What d'ye mean? I worked for Sir Percy for more than twelve years, with no complaints."

"And did you ever insult Lady Wyndham during that time?" Jethro asked.

"No, I never said much to 'er at all," Bennett grunted.

"I can assure you that if you had, he would have done the same as I am doing now," Jethro said. "I'll see you tomorrow, as I said, and pay your final wages. And now, good day to you.''

Bennett stared at him for a moment, as though still unable to believe what had just happened; then he turned and left the room.

Jethro could not say he was sorry for what had occurred, for he had had a distinct feeling from the first that Percy had trusted Bennett too much, and the man had thus become too big for his boots.

As he did not wish to see Sarah just yet, until he had spoken with Sir Malcolm, but felt she should know of his action in case the bailiff should seek to speak with her again, he quickly penned a note to her, telling her briefly what he had done, and saying that he would call on her, with her permission, in the morning. Sealing the missive, he sent a servant to the priory with instructions to put it only into Lady Wyndham's hands.

Then he set out to pay a call on Sir Malcolm Howard.

It was probably going to be a difficult meeting, to say the least, and on the way there, Jethro wondered how he could possibly ask that gentleman if he had been having an affair with his best friend's wife. It was simply not done in the circles in which they moved.

In the event, he was shown into the library, which was decidedly a man's room. The furniture was heavy and glowed with years of loving care, and the books were all carefully categorized. He could have spent several happy hours just looking up favorites of his own.

But it was not even several minutes before Sir Malcolm came in, smiling and with hand outstretched, delighted that he had called and offering him a glass of sherry or something stronger. Because of the matter Jethro had come about, he declined, of course, and they sat down facing each other on either side of the fireplace.

"This is an awkward meeting at best, Sir Malcolm," Jethro said, "but just over a week ago I was told that you and Lady Wyndham were having an affair while Percy was still alive.''

Sir Malcolm looked disbelieving for a moment; then his eyes blazed and he said dangerously quietly, ''How dare you, sir! On that dear lady's behalf, I demand that you retract that statement or name your seconds.''

''I'll do neither, Sir Malcolm, for I simply repeated what I had been told, and I was, in fact, informed that it was common knowledge at the time,'' Jethro said, irritated with the man for jumping to conclusions. ''You must see, sir, that if it were true, it could have a decided effect upon the parentage of the child she is carrying.''

Sir Malcolm came and stood over Jethro, his fists clenched and his face grim.

''I will not deny that I am extremely fond of Sarah, for I think that is quite obvious by now, but I strongly deny that I have shown this in any physical way whatsoever to the dear lady. The child cannot but be Percy's,'' he said emphatically. ''I suppose this is another of Lady Florence's flights of the imagination. She has them quite frequently, you know.''

Jethro nodded.

''What exactly did she tell you, or, more likely, hint at, for she is usually most careful, unless she has been imbibing excessively.''

''She told me that you were a foursome, she with Percy and you with Sarah,'' Jethro told him quietly.

He shook his head emphatically. ''Never! Florence might quite easily have had an affair with Percy before he met Sarah, in fact I had it from a most reliable source that she did, but I can vouch for it that he never even looked at another woman after he became betrothed to Sarah,'' Sir Malcolm stated categorically. ''Does Sarah know that Florence is going about saying such things? She did seem a bit under the weather when I saw her the other day, but with all the problems she's had this last week, I was not one bit surprised.''

"No, she doesn't," Jethro said, "or rather, she doesn't know it's Florence."

"I see," Sir Malcolm said thoughtfully. "However, am I to gather that you have spoken about it to her?"

"Yes, sir. Much to my regret, I broached the matter before I left for London."

"You informed your solicitor of your suspicions, of course?" Sir Malcolm asked, and raised his eyebrows in surprise when Jethro shook his head.

"I couldn't, for by the time I reached London I felt sure that the whole thing was a figment of Florence's imagination, wishful thinking, perhaps, and I could not do anything to harm Sarah's good name," Jethro said sincerely. "You must know that, whether guilty or not, she would have been judged so by the *ton* and would never have been able to hold her head up in London again."

"So the purpose of your visit was to have me refute the suggestions that Florence put into your head regarding Sarah and me?" Sir Malcolm suggested.

"They were more than suggestions, my lord. She had been imbibing rather freely, I am sure, and though I gave her short shrift, she did succeed, I am sorry to say, in putting doubts and fears into my head," Jethro admitted.

"May I renew my offer of sherry?" Sir Malcolm asked. "I can understand your reluctance to accept before, but I believe you and I have some talking to do. Can I also persuade you to stay to dinner if you have no other plans?"

"Thank you, but your cook would no doubt resign if you said you had a guest at this hour, Sir Malcolm. Just throw me out when you're ready to eat and I'll go to my own house for my meat," Jethro said, smiling for the first time since he had entered the house.

"Send a note to the manor and stay," Sir Malcolm said persuasively. "I much prefer company when I dine."

Jethro could not refuse when it was put in that way, and he had, in any case, wanted to get to know the man better—a difficult thing to do in the kind of mixed company where they usually met.

He took out his snuffbox and offered it to his host. "I had time, when in London, to procure some of my favorite blend. Will you try it?"

Sir Malcolm consented, pronounced it exceptional, and wrote down the ingredients. Then he rang for a servant to let Cook know there would be a guest for dinner.

"There's something I've been meaning to mention to you ever since the accident, and as you were away, I did not have the opportunity," he told Jethro when they were comfortably settled once more. "If you recall, the farmer's wife swore that she'd seen that sign in place just before we arrived there."

Jethro nodded. He had a very good idea what Sir Malcolm was going to say, but he did not interrupt.

"You and I went to the carriage to tell Sarah what we were about to do, but Florence rode toward the bridge alone, if I remember correctly. We found the sign lying in a patch of mud, and the post it was fastened to had been snapped in two. The break was fresh, and I put the two parts together. It was just the height for someone on horseback to have given it a good kick. It's impossible to prove, but . . ." He shrugged, leaving the sentence unfinished, the accusation unsaid.

"I should not like to think it deliberate," Jethro said, "but more likely a momentary desire to kick at something because you and I were giving the other ladies our attention. And as you say, there is no proof." He shrugged. "Fortunately, only the carriage suffered as a consequence."

Sir Malcolm looked at him closely. "Then you've not been to the priory since your return?"

Startled, Jethro said quickly, "No, I have not, for I reached the manor only late this afternoon. Is something wrong with Sarah?"

"Not with Sarah," Sir Malcolm reassured him, "other than being worn to a thread, for even our good Dr. Unwin could not persuade her to get some rest and let the servants nurse Lady Ramsbottom. You see, the soaking the old lady received took effect on her a couple of days later, and she came down with a severe inflammation of the lungs—a most dangerous condition for one of her advanced years.''

"How is she doing?" Jethro asked quickly.

"Remarkably well now, I understand, considering everything," Sir Malcolm told him, "but don't go haring off to the priory right away, for there's nothing you can do tonight. Dr. Unwin has brought his own nurse to tend to Lady Ramsbottom during the night, when she seems to be the most uncomfortable, so Sarah will be trying to get some well-earned rest this evening.''

"I'll go over there first thing in the morning, and I would like to have a word with that doctor. Have you any idea when he usually calls and what he is like?" Jethro asked, remembering that he had meant to make sure Sarah was in the hands of a good man.

"He's an excellent man, too good really for a country practice. I really don't know his visiting hours, but would imagine he will be coming in the afternoon once the old lady is going along fairly well. And now, sir, shall we go into the dining room and see what my cook has been able to provide for our delectation? One finds, as one gets older, that good food, good wine, and good company assume a much greater importance than they ever did before.''

He rose, and Jethro followed him into an elegant, if old-fashioned, dining room where a fire burned brightly in the hearth and the warm glow of a couple of dozen candles revealed enough food and delicacies for a dozen or more guests.

"My cook is so happy to have another dinner guest that she overreaches herself, I'm afraid," Sir Malcolm remarked as footmen seated the two of them and the butler poured a little of the wine for his master to taste. "Just right," he murmured, motioning for him to pour a glass for their guest. "What do you think, Jethro?"

There was no question about the fact that Sir Malcolm set a quite excellent table, and Jethro could not recall when he had enjoyed a better meal.

"Do you find you miss the comradeship of life in the army, Jethro?" Sir Malcolm asked. "You were with Wellington for quite a number of years, I believe."

"Five, to be exact, and yes, there have been times when I wondered what they were doing and wished I was there. I have found, though, that it's not exactly difficult for one to grow accustomed to a roof over one's head every single night, dry feather beds to sleep on instead of flea-infested mattresses, and enough food at one meal to feed a whole battalion." He grinned. "However, I wouldn't have missed those years for anything in the world."

"You have a most decided flair for leadership, which I noticed to my chagrin at that bridge last week," Sir Malcolm said with a somewhat reluctant admiration. "One could almost see the idea ticking in your head as you gathered the helpers together into a workable team. I heard that you were on a leave of absence only. Do you have plans to return eventually?"

Jethro shook his head. "Certainly not to the Peninsula, for my regiment is already in France, but I would very much doubt that I shall return to the army at all. Much depends, however, on what I find tomorrow morning."

There was a bleak expression in Sir Malcolm's eyes. "I cannot in all honesty wish you success, for I love her as much as you do, but if you win her, you had better make her happy or you'll have to answer to me," he said very quietly.

"I shall do my very best, sir," was all Jethro would promise.

"And now, my lord, can I offer you a taste of a very fine port?" Sir Malcolm suggested—the perfect host once more.

"Why not?" Jethro asked. "It would be an excellent ending to a quite outstanding meal."

"I'll make sure that word gets back to Cook," Sir Malcolm said with a grin. "Shall we have it in the library?"

They returned to the comfortable man-sized chairs and sipped their port as they talked about the merits of Eton versus Harrow and Oxford versus Cambridge, and, like the excellent host he was, Sir Malcolm did not bring up the subject of hunting. Then Jethro reluctantly rose to take his leave.

"My thanks again for a delicious dinner and one of the most pleasant informal evenings I can recall having spent in a long time," Jethro said, clasping Sir Malcolm's hand in a firm grip. "If I invite you to dine with me at the priory, will you come?"

"The priory?" Sir Malcolm looked puzzled.

"I intend to move Sarah back to the manor as soon as possible," Jethro said, "for her child should be born there."

Sir Malcolm smiled and nodded, pleased with the idea, and with the man, despite the rivalry between them. "I'll most certainly come and dine with you, Jethro. Give my best wishes to Sarah when you see her."

Jethro's carriage was waiting for him outside, and it was not more than ten minutes later that he was back at Mansfield Manor. Dismissing the carriage, he entered the house and went up to his bedchamber, where, without waking the sleeping Bridges, he quickly changed from evening shoes into a more serviceable pair of walking shoes. Then he left the house once more and started walking slowly down the lane that led to the priory.

He approached the building quietly, not wishing to disturb anyone but just needing to see if everything looked all right, he told himself.

"Who is it? Who's out there?"

There was no mistaking her low voice, and Jethro stood where he was, trying to see where she was. He wondered what she was doing outside at this hour.

"It's Jethro, Sarah," he called softly, hoping she would be able to hear him; then he knew she had, for he could see her slight figure moving toward him.

He moved also, and when they were within a yard of each other, they both halted.

He did not speak or go any further forward, but he held out his arms and a moment later she was in them, her head pressed against his shoulder and one of his hands stroking her soft brown hair.

Later, he could not have told anyone how long she remained like that, but when she raised her head there were tears on her cheeks that he gently wiped away with his fingers.

"It's been the most dreadful week, Jethro," she murmured. "First that awful quarrel with you, and then Aunt Agatha was so sick that I thought she might not survive."

"How is she now?" he asked gently.

"Much better than she was, but now we have to make sure that there's no permanent damage. And I feel dreadful, for in a way it was my fault she took ill. Because I was upset, I didn't notice that she was not at all well," she said sadly.

His hands framed her lovely face. "You know that it's nothing of the sort," he said softly, "and I'm sure you've done far more than you should have to look after her. How do you feel?"

"Terribly tired still, but much better as soon as I got your note about that awful man. I was so glad you came back, and most grateful that you got rid of him, but what will you do?" Her soft voice sounded much stronger now.

"We'll find someone else, don't worry about it. Sir Malcolm sent his regards," he told her.

"He had a dinner party tonight?" She sounded mildly curious.

"No, it was just the two of us—and I wasn't invited, not in advance anyway." His mouth was so close to the top of her head that his breath blew wisps of her hair as he spoke. "We'll talk about it tomorrow, but tonight I just want to tell you how very much I have regretted all those dreadful things I said to you. I stayed away longer than I meant to, for I was afraid it might be some time before you would forgive me.''

"I'm not sure if I am going to forgive you right away," she murmured. "I should make you suffer a little first for hurting me so, but I wanted to see you tonight so very much.''

"You may do your worst, my dear," he said softly, "as long as I know you will forgive me in the end.''

She could feel his breath on her forehead as he spoke, and then his lips lightly touched the same spot and she gave a little shiver of delight.

"Are you feeling better now? No aftereffects from the accident?" he asked.

She nodded. "I'm becoming very sleepy, though. I couldn't sleep earlier, because I was too tired. Does that make sense?''

He smiled down at her. "A great deal of sense, for that often happens when you overdo. Let me take you to the door now. Do you think you can manage the stairs?''

She nodded again. "Yes. Will I see you in the morning?''

"I'll be here, I promise," he murmured. "Now, get some sleep.''

His lips barely touched her forehead; then he pushed her gently through the door and closed it quietly behind her, waiting until he heard her slide the bolts home.

Only then did he turn and walk slowly back to the manor, reliving that strange dreamlike meeting. He, too, would sleep now, he knew, for everything was going to be all right.

18

The following morning Jethro went into the library even before entering the breakfast room, and sent word by a footman that he wished to see both Mrs. Pennyfarthing and Rivers.

While he waited for them to appear, he went carefully through the drawers of the desk, removing anything of a strictly personal nature, and by the time he had finished they were just inside the door, awaiting his pleasure with not a little trepidation.

"Please be seated," he said quietly, "for there is something I wish to explain to you both, in confidence, in order that you may quash any strange rumors that may start to circulate belowstairs."

With a rather pained expression, for he really did not approve of such informality, Rivers picked up a straight chair from the side of the room and placed it in front of the desk for Mrs. Pennyfarthing, then went back to get one for himself. Only when they were both seated, though somewhat uncomfortably on the very edges of the chairs, did Jethro continue.

"You probably know already that yesterday I gave Jim Bennett his marching orders," he said quietly, "and you have only his version of why this took place after so many years of, as he said, loyal service to the family."

Rivers inclined his head, but Mrs. Pennyfarthing appeared to be quite startled.

"I have to admit that I have not found his work satisfactory since I came here, but would have told him so and given him a chance to improve had he not been, on his own admission, disrespectful to Lady Wyndham. He did not feel he need take orders from her, and told her so."

Mrs. Pennyfarthing gave a little gasp, and murmured, "How dare he?" Rivers' face remained impassive but his eyes revealed his disgust, for they were both very fond of her ladyship.

"I can fully understand that it has been difficult for the staff to know who was actually in charge, and I had assumed that you would have instructed them to do everything they were told by either her ladyship or by me." He paused as both heads nodded in confirmation.

He gave them a twisted grin. "I'm afraid the situation has now become somewhat more complicated, for though her ladyship is not yet aware of it, we are changing residences. Just as soon as Lady Ramsbottom is fit to be moved, I will go to live at the priory and the two ladies will return here, with whatever staff we decide upon, of course. I want you to make doubly sure that her ladyship takes the very best possible care of herself. Have you any idea what doctor she consults, Mrs. Pennyfarthing?"

The housekeeper shook her head. "No, milord, I have not, for she was never in need of a doctor when she was here, nor have I heard that one's been to see her at the priory either, unless Dr. Unwin has said something to her when he came to Lady Ramsbottom."

Jethro sighed. "I had a feeling such was the case, and I will speak to her about it today. What I'd like you to do at once it to put the master bedchamber back the way it was before I arrived here, so that Lady Wyndham may be as comfortable as possible. She will remain here at least until her child is born.'' He heard a sigh of relief from Mrs. Pennyfarthing, but went on. ''My valet is at this moment moving my belongings into an adjacent bedchamber so that the master bedchamber can be prepared, and I will stay only until the ladies can make the move. I'm sure I have no need to tell you that I will expect the staff to obey their wishes to the letter. Is that clear?''

''It's just what we have been doing, milord, all along,'' Mrs. Pennyfarthing asserted. ''Only someone as forward as that bailiff, Bennett, would have thought of anything else.''

River inclined his head in complete agreement.

''Has either of you any questions?''

The housekeeper glanced at Rivers, quite obviously hoping he would ask the question that was on the tip of her tongue, but he was far too well-trained to do so.

She heaved a sigh, then asked, ''I don't mean to be disrespectful, milord, but I wondered if we are still to speak of you as the earl?''

Jethro's eyes twinkled. ''Not at the moment,'' he said, ''and as for the future, it depends on whether Lady Wyndham gives birth to a son or a daughter. If it's a son, then he will immediately be the new earl.''

The smile on the housekeeper's face showed her complete approval. ''And if it's a girl, then you take over?'' she asked.

''Precisely, Mrs. Pennyfarthing,'' Jethro said, bearing the loyal retainer no grudge for her obvious preference. ''Are there any other questions? Rivers?''

''No, milord,'' the butler said calmly.

''Then you may start preparations for the ladies' arrival, and as soon as I have had some breakfast, I will go to the priory and tell them of the plans. I would seriously doubt, however, that Lady Wyndham will object to the changeover.''

After replacing the chairs at the side of the room, the two servants left to go about their business, but Jethro sat for a moment recalling his meeting last night with Sarah and wondering what today's meeting would bring. Then he rose and made his way to the breakfast room, but was too impatient to do more than nibble on a piece of toast and an egg. Then he left on foot for the priory.

George looked somewhat relieved to see the earl, and showed him at once into the dining room, where Sarah sat alone, and she, too, was just nibbling on a piece of toast and pushing some egg around on a plate.

She looked up and smiled with a little uncertainty. "Good morning, Jethro. Did you have breakfast yet?"

"I had something before I left," he told her, smiling gently, "but if you'll try to eat a little more, then so will I."

She nodded to George, who gave her a fresh plate of bacon and eggs, then made up a similar plate for his lordship before leaving the room and closing the door behind him.

"How is Lady Ramsbottom this morning?" Jethro asked. "Did she have a good night?"

"The nurse said she seemed a little better than the night before, but we'll find out more when Dr. Unwin arrives," she told him, taking a forkful of eggs and eating them without even noticing. "You must have been tired last night after your journey. Did you sleep well?"

He inclined his head, not taking his eyes off her. "I did after I'd seen you," he said, then asked, "And you? Did you sleep well?"

She smiled. "I had the best night's sleep I've had all week," she admitted. "I felt better also."

"I'm glad," he murmured, then looked at her with troubled eyes. "I hardly know how to begin to tell you how sorry I am for the things I said before I left for London. I—"

She leaned forward. "Please don't," she begged, forgetting her friend, Lillian's admonitions to make him pay for his behavior. "You said all that was necessary last evening, in fact we both said things we didn't mean, and I'd much rather put it behind me and start afresh. Wouldn't you?"

His smile warmed her as nothing else could have done, and he reached out and placed one of his hands over hers.

"Of course, though you are being much kinder than I deserve."

They looked at each other for a long moment; then Jethro grinned. "I'd better tell you now what our respective solicitors had to say. Surprisingly, they're in agreement that should you have a boy, he will inherit the earldom at once, and that you should move back into the manor as soon as possible, for the child should be born there. Mrs. Pennyfarthing is already preparing the master suite for you, and as soon as Lady Ramsbottom is well enough, we'll make the changeover."

"I'm not sure what you mean," Sarah told him, hoping that he meant he would stay here, but not daring to take it for granted.

"Just that I'll move in with the ghosts over here," he said with a grin. "One thing Mr. Musgrave asked me is if you planned to call in a London doctor for the birth, but I said I did not recall your having seen a doctor."

"I have now," she told him rather sheepishly. "When Dr. Unwin saw my condition, he insisted on checking to be sure everything was going along all right. He was Percy's doctor, you know, and a friend of the family."

Jethro heaved a sigh of relief. "And you're going to let him check you regularly?" he asked.

She nodded, smiling mischievously. "He threatens to come out here once a month if I don't keep in close touch with him."

"That's one problem off of my mind, anyway," Jethro said, then asked, "Do you think I might be able to see Lady Ramsbottom, or is she still too sick as yet?"

"I'm sure you could if you want to," Sarah said, frowning a little, "but she can't talk much, you know."

"That's all right, for I mean to do all the talking, but I won't tire her, I promise." Jethro looked at her plate, which was, surprisingly, quite empty.

"Your good influence," she said, smiling. "If you'd like

to come up with me now, I'll see if she's awake and relieve the nurse who has been on duty all night.''

They went quietly up the stairs and into her aunt's bed-chamber. Jethro looked around him at what once had quite obviously been two bedchambers when the priory was first built. Even after a wall had been removed the room was large enough for only the canopied bed, a small dressing table and a chair, and an armoire. For a man of his size to sit beside the bed, he had to ease his way in first and then pull the chair after him, which procedure he now performed.

The old lady was propped up by pillows, and her eyes were wide open, but she looked terribly old and much frailer than she had a week ago.

A wrinkled hand lay on the counterpane, and he took it in his two large ones, and though she frowned at him, she did not attempt to withdraw the hand.

''I just wanted to tell you myself that as soon as you're able, you are both to move back to the manor so that Sarah can have her baby there,'' he said quietly.

She nodded slowly; then he leaned forward to hear what she was trying to say. ''You made your peace with her, did you?''

He nodded, and a small spark came into the tired old eyes. ''You going to wed her?'' she asked, her voice barely a whisper.

''If she'll have me,'' he told her quietly.

She smiled then and closed her eyes as her hand slipped out of his.

Unknown to him, Sarah had been standing behind him, making sure that her aunt did not become too tired, and she slipped quietly away before he moved from the bed, embarrassed to have overheard the brief conversation, but not at all unhappy about it. She had been sure now for more than a week that she was in love with him, for she could not possibly have been so upset by his accusations had she not been.

Now all she needed to do was make sure that he loved her

in return, because she had no father this time to scoff at such ideas and tell her she must do her duty.

Would he ask her now, she wondered, or would he wait until the child was born before doing so? And would it really be wrong to marry again before she was out of mourning for Percy?

"Dr. Unwin will be here soon," she told Jethro when he had squeezed his way out of her aunt's chamber, "and I want to give her a drink of barley water now, for I believe her throat is parched."

"I would like a word with the doctor, so I'll wait downstairs for his arrival," he said quietly. "After that, I must ride out and make sure Bennett is making no mischief on his last day here. May I join you for dinner tonight, at whatever time you suggest?"

She smiled, pleased that he had invited himself. "Would half-past six be all right? The nurse will be relieving me at six and it will give me time to change."

He was only just beginning to realize what a great number of problems she was carrying on those small shoulders. "I'll talk to Cook myself and plan it, if you like," he said, "and the sooner we get Lady Ramsbottom over to the manor, the better it will be, for there's not room enough to swing a cat around in there."

"That is one of the larger rooms," she told him. "You should see mine."

He grinned. "I'd be delighted to," he said, and watched the flush of embarrassment that stained her cheeks. "I'm sorry, I just couldn't resist teasing you. I'll see you tonight at about half-past six."

He slipped out quietly and was halfway down the stairs when he heard a strange voice in the hall and realized it must be Dr. Unwin.

"Dr. Unwin? I am Jethro Newsome, and I wonder if I might have a word with you before you go to see your patient," he requested, clasping the doctor's hand in a firm grip, then leading him into the small back room.

"I'm glad to find you've returned, my lord," the doctor said, "for though Lady Wyndham is most capable, she is inclined to try to do everything herself, and I'm afraid that, particularly in her present condition, it is not a very good idea."

"I'm glad we're in complete agreement, sir," Jethro said pleasantly, offering him a chair near the fireplace and taking the one opposite for himself. "How soon do you think it might be possible to move Lady Ramsbottom to the manor? I meant to do so, in any case, but when I saw the size of the bedchamber, I realized how much better she would be in a larger, airy room."

Dr. Unwin was a man of medium height, about forty years of age, with sandy hair and blue eyes that could be piercing if the need arose. He had a firm, no-nonsense mouth, and Jethro had taken an instant liking to him.

"I could not agree with you more, and I cannot for the life of me understand why they moved over to the priory in the first place," the doctor said bluntly.

"Lady Wyndham was unaware that she carried the earl's child when she made the arrangements to live here, just before I got here," Jethro informed him, "and I have told her this morning that she is to return there just as soon as the old lady can be moved. Her child must be born at Mansfield Manor."

Dr. Unwin grinned. "I hope she takes more kindly to your orders than she does to mine," he said, "but I would say that in a couple of days, if my patient is carefully wrapped in blankets and taken over in the middle of the afternoon, when it's warmer, she should come to no harm. You can't even get a halfway decent fire going in the chamber she's in now."

Jethro nodded in agreement. "I see now that the place is fit only for what it was originally intended, a residence for monks," he said. "And now for the other matter I wanted to discuss with you, sir. Lady Wyndham's solicitor was all for bringing in a London doctor for the birthing, but I don't think she would take kindly to a strange man. You appear to be most capable, and honest enough, I believe, to bring in someone else if it should prove necessary.''

"I doubt if it will come to that," the doctor said, a little put out by the reference to a London doctor. "When I found that she'd seen no one, I insisted on taking a look at her, and she seems to be in the best of health. But as you say, I'd not take any chances on handling it alone if there were complications, so you needn't worry. Your interest is, of course, as head of the family?''

Jethro smiled a little apologetically. "That and the fact that I mean to marry her as soon as she is out of mourning, if she will have me.''

"I'd do it before, if I were you," the doctor said bluntly. "You're not in London, where people feel they can dictate what you should do. The best time would be before the child is born, for women are inclined to get a little depressed when it's all over and the baby is here. But that advice is free and completely up to you, of course. And now I'd best see how Lady Ramsbottom is doing today.''

They rose and left the room, the doctor to take the stairs two at a time, and Jethro to return to the kitchen, where he made arrangements for a very special dinner to be prepared and served that evening.

It was with a feeling of satisfaction that he returned to the manor, then rode off, a little later, to see how some of the improvements he had put into effect had fared during the week he had been absent. He found, as he had feared, that a bailiff who shirked his duties and an absentee landlord were a poor combination even for so short a period, and by late afternoon he had been glad to pay off Bennett and be rid of him, and had selected someone to fill in until he could procure a first-class man for the job.

Before getting out of his dusty clothes, he went along to the master suite to see what progress had been made. As he expected, everything appeared to be in readiness in the lady's bedchamber and in the sitting room that divided it from the

gentleman's. Then his eye caught something that he knew
had not been there before. A few feet from the four-poster
bed was a beautifully carved cradle, not new by any means,
but polished till it glowed, and fitted with tiny snowy white
pillows and sheets edged in lace.

There was a tap on the open door and he turned to see
Mrs. Pennyfarthing standing there.

"It's all ready for her, my lord," she said. "Do you think
she'll like it?"

"She cannot but like it," he told her, smiling. "Was this
your doing?" He pointed to the cradle.

"The cradle was in the attic, but the staff have been making
baby things for her ladyship ever since they first heard she
was in the family way." She was beaming with pride. "She
doesn't know, of course."

"She will be delighted, I am sure, and will thank each and
every one of them personally, if I know anything. I spoke
to the doctor and he feels that Lady Ramsbottom will be fit
to be carefully moved in a couple of days. So it won't be
long before you have your mistress back, Mrs. Pennyfarthing, and the staff at the priory will have to put up with me,"
he said, and could not help chuckling ata her discomfiture.

"My goodness, milord, you surely know I didn't mean
it that way, but you must realize that we've all grown so
very fond of her ladyship," she said, then realized she was
only making things worse.

He left her standing there, her round face red with embarrassment, and returned to the small chamber he was using
for the time being, where Bridges waited with a steaming
tub of hot water and his evening clothes laid out ready for
him.

He whistled softly to himself as he scrubbed himself
thoroughly, for he had never wanted a servant to perform
such tasks for him. Then he vigorously toweled himself dry
before submitting to the ministrations of Bridges for all else
save the tying of his cravat, which he was far too particular
about to leave to his man's clumsy fingers. He grinned

happily when his first attempt was a complete success, and gave Bridges a mock salute as he closed the door behind him.

A few minutes later, as he started out for the priory, his courage suddenly deserted him. What if she preferred to wait until the child was born before deciding whether to marry him or not? Was it possible he had misread her feelings? Might she just turn him down out of hand?

The colonel who had confidently led his troops to victory on so many occasions was suddenly unsure that this time he would come away the winner.

19

As soon as Jethro was announced, Sarah rose and went forward to greet him. Jethro took her outstretched hand in his and bowed low, touching it lightly with his lips. Then he led her over to the chair she favored these days, and brought her a small glass of sherry.

"You look very beautiful tonight, and a little more rested, I believe," he told her. "How is Lady Ramsbottom feeling?"

"Much better, and looking forward to the move back to Mansfield Manor," she said, her gaze determinedly fixed on a point between his exquisitely tied cravat and the lowest ruffle of his snowy white shirt. It was a ploy most necessary, for, as if of their own volition, her eyes kept straying to the fascinating movement of the muscles of his thighs beneath his clinging knee breeches.

He looked down at his shirt, then back to her with puzzlement. "If there's a spot that my batman missed, I'll have his hide," he promised, but when her cheeks turned a becoming pink, he quickly changed the subject. "Did Cook reveal to you what we're having for dinner tonight?"

She shook her head. "She refused to tell me, for she thought it was to be a surprise, but she did say it was very special. I hope it will be cooked to your liking, though, for she's not to be compared with the cook at the manor."

It was of no consequence insofar as he was concerned, and he said lightly, "I spent too many years with little thought for what the next meal might consist of, let alone taste like, to worry. The peasants had little enough for themselves, without trying to feed an army, though we did, for the most part, pay for our food. But I have a feeling that your cook might indeed outdo herself this evening and agreeably surprise you."

Her eyes twinkled as she murmured, "I hope so, for when you have gone to so much trouble, I would not like her to disappoint you. I do not recall anyone ever planning a surprise dinner just for me, even for my birthday, which is still many months away."

The light in her eyes dimmed a little as she thought how strange her birthday would feel this year without Percy; then she realized that Jethro had been saying something else, which she had missed.

"Please forgive me," she begged. "My mind wandered for a moment."

"Oh course, my dear," he said, his smile so very understanding that she felt sure he knew what she had been thinking of. "I was just saying that it's more than possible you will regret your move to the manor. The staff are so pleased you are returning that they will probably fuss and coddle you until you'll wish to make frequent visits here purely as a means of escape."

At least I can use it as an excuse to come here and see how he is going along, Sarah thought. "They're all very good and extremely well-trained," she said aloud, "and, you know, Mrs. Pennyfarthing has been with the family since she was a tweeny."

He laughed aloud. "I cannot imagine that good but large lady ever being small enough for such a title, but she will, I am sure, take the best possible care of you."

There was the sound of George clearing his throat before announcing that dinner was served, and Jethro jumped up quickly and offered Sarah his arm.

Now, beneath the fabric of his coat, she could actually feel some of those muscles, and she was surprised at how hard they were. She realized that this was the first time she had ever dined completely alone with a man to whom she was not closely related by blood or marriage, but it did not feel at all strange. On the contrary, it seemed the most natural thing in the world to do. He did appear to be a little nervous this evening, though, and she could not help but wonder if this was to be the first of many such evenings or if he had a special purpose in planning it so carefully.

Once he had seated her across from himself, and the many dishes of the first course had been placed in front of them, Jethro thanked George and told him they would help themselves and ring when they were ready for the next course. A delicious turtle soup was followed by salmon and turbot, with a little tongue, ham, roast woodcock, and potted lamprey. Asparagus, peas, stewed mushrooms, and potatoes accompanied the meats, and then figs, dates, peaches, and bananas were served with custards and puff pastries.

Though quite small when judged beside the usual London dinners, it was a large meal compared to the ones Sarah usually ate at home.

"The turbot has an exceptionally fine sauce," Jethro remarked. "Allow me to put a little on your plate."

She passed her plate to him and his fingers touched her hand as he took it from her, and again when he gave it back, sending warm, tingling sensations up her arm.

After that, he insisted on serving her small amounts of each dish, and it seemed that his hands constantly touched her own as he handed her plates of fresh foods to sample, or peeled a piece of fruit for her.

By the time tea had been brought to her and Jethro's port was placed before him, she felt quite light-headed, not from the wine, for this she had scarcely touched, but from his closeness and his particular attention to her every need. Of late she had begun to feel a little heavy and awkward with the child she carried, but this evening he made her feel graceful and attractive again. His eyes were speaking to her in a way no one else's ever had, and saying things she hoped they really meant.

He reached across the table and clasped her hand, then stroked it lightly with just the tips of his fingers. Next, those fingers circled her palm, and she found herself breathless and confused, wanting something she had never known.

And all the time his eyes looked into hers, at first kindly and comforting, but now she was sure she could see a deep passion within their depths.

"It's a warm evening," he said huskily, a slightly lopsided grin creasing a corner of his mouth. "Would you like to send for a wrap and go for a stroll with me to walk off some of that excellent dinner? You really must admit that everything was cooked to perfection."

"I'll readily admit it, and cannot help wondering what you said to the cook to bring about such an improvement. If you'll excuse me, I'll go up and get a wrap myself," she told him softly. "Shall I meet you here?"

"Where else?" he asked, grinning so broadly that she had to wonder if perhaps she was walking into some kind of trap. But she did not care, for she knew without the slightest doubt that he would never do her harm.

She had to remind herself not to run up the stairs, as she would have done some months ago. Instead, she walked up them quite sedately, picking up a shawl in her small bed-chamber and pausing also to change from the light slippers she was wearing to a more serviceable pair.

When she returned, he was standing in the same spot as she had left him, and he took the shawl from her hands and wrapped it securely around her shoulders, then held his arm out to escort her.

George's face was as impassive as the best-trained London butler's might be as he held the front door for them to pass through, closing it quietly behind them. It seemed dark at first, so they kept to the private road and walked slowly in the direction of the manor, though not intending to go quite so far.

Jethro's arm was about her now, making sure she did not stumble or trip in the darkness. Surprisingly, his did not feel at all strange to Sarah but comfortable and oddly familiar.

Suddenly he chuckled, the sound echoing a little in the quiet of the night, and Sarah said curiously, "I do hope you're laughing at yourself and not at me."

She felt his arm tighten around her.

"Never at you, my love," he assured her, and was silent for a moment, then said, "I was just thinking of how you looked when I first met you, and how eager I was to know you better. I never dreamed that you were Percy's widow, but thought you must be his stepdaughter or some other relative. Then, before the evening was over, I decided you were a veritable spitfire, a shrew who had probably driven Percy into an early grave."

Sarah laughed, recalling the things she had said to him that night.

"I never thought that I would grow to love you so much that the estates, title, money, don't matter as long as I can be near you." He stopped, and turned so that he could look into her upturned face. "Will you marry me, Sarah? Not right away, if you feel it's too soon after Percy's death. I'll wait to marry, if need be, until after the baby is born, but I cannot wait for your answer. I need to know now if my feelings are reciprocated."

She turned her face away, and her voice was muffled at first; then quite distinctly she said, "Of course I will marry you, Jethro. You surely d-don't think I would let you take me for a walk at this hour if I d-didn't mean to marry you."

He put a finger beneath her chin and made her look at him again, then realized why she had turned away, for her face was wet with tears.

"D-don't look like that, you oaf," she said. "You should know by now that I c-cry only in public when I'm happy."

Jethro was trying not to laugh, but a grin still sneaked out. As if to make up for it, he withdrew a handkerchief and wiped her face, then waited while she blew her nose hard.

"I do remember," he said softly, and pulled her gently back into his arms.

She knew he must feel the roundness of the child between them, for he was careful not to squeeze her tightly. Then his mouth traced a slow, delicate pattern from her forehead downward, teasing and caressing until finally his lips found hers and Sarah realized, as she felt a fire begin to smolder inside her, that she had known nothing about love and loving until this moment.

Her own lips parted quite naturally when his tongue demanded entrance. Then, as it went deeper into the moist depths, alternately tasting and demanding, she felt aflame and mindless, living only through her senses, which absorbed the new sensations and begged for more.

She felt rather than heard his deep sigh, and only then realized that her hands had been massaging the muscles of his back and drawing him closer in a desperate need she had never thought to know.

"Are you all right?" he asked a moment later. "I didn't hurt you, did I?"

She shook her head happily. "No, of course you didn't, but I've never felt like that before," she said, feeling not embarrassed in the slightest at her own unrestrained response.

"Neither have I," he told her honestly, "and I only wish we did not have to wait to get married. Let's start back, for the last thing I want is for you to catch a chill."

Sarah still felt so warm that she could not imagine such a thing happening, but she took his outstretched hand and they started to retrace their steps.

"You will be like a father to Percy's child, won't you?" she asked suddenly, though she knew full well what his answer would be.

"Of course. How else could I behave? Whether it's a boy or a girl is no matter—only that it's healthy. And it will not be lonely or spoiled, for I mean to make sure it has many siblings,'' he told her, giving her a look so warm that she moved closer and was immediately clasped in his arms again.

After some time she asked, ''Do you think it will give rise to much speculation if we get married before I'm out of mourning?''

''Yes, I am sure it will, and I think there'll be just as much if we wait until your child is born, for people will think that I wanted to secure my own interests if it's a boy; and if it's a girl, they'll say you wanted to retain your position as Countess of Mansfield rather than be the dowager.'' He sighed. ''Does it matter to you what people think?''

''I hate to admit it,'' Sarah said ruefully, ''but it does, for gossip can be so damaging to one's reputation. It would seem that the only time best for both of us would be just before the baby comes. Perhaps we could put an announcement in the *Gazette* now, and then marry quietly when we feel it appropriate?''

''If by quietly you mean by special license, I think it a sound idea, for the announcement will stop most people reading something into it that is not there,'' he said thoughtfully. ''I think you must be prepared, though, to meet with disapproval from the high sticklers, no matter what we do.''

''Of course,'' she agreed, ''but they will not dare to offend you, and I am in town so infrequently that it will be of no consequence to me.''

''What will your stepmama say, I wonder. There is no possible way that I will allow you to go to town without me and help with her daughter's come-out,'' he told her, grinning.

''She'll not care as long as you permit her to use the Mansfield town house and pay for all the gowns and, of course, for the come-out ball,'' Sarah informed him.

''I'll probably meet her halfway,'' he said agreeably. ''I don't believe I told you that my mama is in town right now helping her sister bring out my cousin. She's very eager to meet you, so I'll invite her down next weekend, if that's all right with you.''

As far as Sarah was concerned, she was so very happy that anything would have been all right with her, and with Jethro at her side, she would look forward to the weeks and months and years ahead with joyful anticipation.

Two and a half months later, in a simple ceremony in the drawing room at Mansfield Manor, the dowager Lady Wyndham and Viscount Jethro Newsome were married by the local vicar.

The bride wore a simple gown of dove gray and, at her insistence, the bridegroom was resplendent in his scarlet-and-blue dress uniform. Everyone agreed that Sarah had never looked lovelier or happier.

Their close friends Sir Malcolm Howard and Mrs. Lillian Lofthouse were the witnesses, and Lord Robert Pelham gave the bride away. Also present were Lady Agatha Ramsbottom and Mr. Edward Lofthouse.

In view of Sarah's condition, they had, fortunately, postponed indefinitely their wedding trip, for, just three days later, she gave birth to a beautiful baby girl with soft fiery red hair and blue eyes that already held a hint of the green of Lord Percy's. In time the child would have brothers, one of whom would succeed his father, now Lord Jethro Newsome, Earl of Mansfield, but she would always hold a very special place in the hearts of her parents.